DR. FRANKS AND
THE ANTMEN

Chris Bittler

Bad Idea Books

badideabooks.com

For Kildare Wilson.

CONTENTS

EXCELSIOR

Sergeant Marvin Dingle stood outside the crime scene, glancing both ways down the busy New York street. Sometimes downtown then up, sometimes uptown then down. So far Dingle had counted thirty-four taxis and seven men in red berets. There wasn't much else to do. Mostly Sergeant Dingle looked directly across the street, at a viola in the window of Flavin's Music Emporium. As a younger man, Dingle had dreams of being a concert violist. Or was it violaist? True, his instructor at the Julliard Annex (not affiliated with the Julliard) was not optimistic, but Wendell Stern, half-brother of Isaac, whom Dingle had met in Central Park and to whom he had lent five bucks for the purchase of some after-dinner cough syrup, had insisted Dingle was "aces." Alas, a wife and a baby had pushed Dingle into the family trade of police work—more so the wife than the baby, which tended to keep its opinions to itself.

Dingle let out a tiny sigh. He knew that his dreams of musical greatness were behind him, as were the others: the wire jewelry business, the pro wrestling career and the sheep farm in Australia. No, it was definitely time to focus on advancing in his current vocation. Countless lectures from his wife had drilled into him the notion that he could make detective if he only applied himself. And at times like these, standing outside a crime scene with nothing to do but count taxis and red berets, his beloved's shrill and frequent dinner remonstrations thumped inside his cranium like a nagging sinus infection. Perhaps, he now thought, today was his chance to prove himself. Perhaps, without access to the clues and using only his intuition and knowledge of human nature, he, Sergeant Marvin Dingle, could solve this case. Like Charlie Chan or Father Brown. Yes, he would do it! He would determine the cause of the death (or deaths—he had not, after all, been allowed into the accident scene itself) single-handedly. Then they'd make him detective, and that would show his wife! All he had to do was focus and not let his mind wander as it so often did.

Milliseconds later, his eye was drawn to a shiny object in the street. A quarter! Which reminded him of another dream— that of starting his own combination laundromat and vendorama or, as he had hoped to call it, a laundrovendoramamat. Bending down to pick up the coin he failed to notice the thirty-fifth taxi. Which ran him over. The cabbie was wearing a red beret, which would have made eight for the day had Dingle seen him. But he didn't what with being run over and all.

Inside, five men and a woman stood in the small supply room of the Excelsior Bowling Apparel Co. Ltd. Or rather, four men and a woman were standing, looking down at the sixth occupant, who lay face up on the floor, his upper torso half-hidden by a large mimeograph machine. The unnatural positioning of the man's legs, reminiscent of a grasshopper sporting wingtips, was a solid clue that he would not be joining the rest of the group in conversation.

Two of the men, New York's finest, stood with their backs to the door to keep out the knot of curious employees. A third, Inspector Grimes, had positioned himself at one corner of a triangle, the other points anchored by the victim and a voluptuous young blonde by the name of Miss Chanelle. Grimes had been scribbling furiously in his pocket notebook.

"You knew Mr. Mishnik?"

"Of course," Miss Chanelle said. "He's been Excelsior's accountant for as long as anyone can remember."

"And yet you don't seem too broken up by his death."

Miss Chanelle's eyes widened. Her porcelain cheeks flashed crimson.

"I don't know what you are implying."

Grimes eyed her with suspicion. He eyed everyone with suspicion. "You were not intimate with the deceased? You had no reason to wish him harm?"

Miss Chanelle seemed insulted. "Intimate? With little Mr. Mishnik? I mean, lately he had been asking me out, but of course I declined. He was," she glanced quickly at the visible portion of the corpse—short legs covered with mismatched socks and brown slacks worn at the knees, "not my type." Then she pursed her lips as if about to cry. The two coppers quickly offered hankies, but she brushed them aside and turned toward the door. Grimes was about to say something, but the fourth living man in the room, who had been silent until now, stayed him with a wave.

"Let her go," he said in a slight British accent.

The four living men paused to watch her walk through the knot of co-workers, which simultaneously parted and turned to watch her walk. She had a great walk.

"Dr. Franks," Grimes said at last, "I wish you'd let me run my own investigation." For that is who the fourth man was. The famous Dr. Benjamin Franks: explorer, philosopher and inventor of the electric can opener. Franks was a large man of regal bearing, despite the scraggly gray beard and impossibly-wrinkled putty raincoat. The corn flakes on his shirt didn't help either. Nor the Zagnut wrapper sticking out of his pocket. But it was the great man's eyes that demanded attention. Those crazy, googily eyes.

Chris Bittler

"She definitely did not have a relationship with our Mr. Mishnik," Franks said. "She's a quite a tootsie and our late accountant was more of a Tootsie Roll."

Grimes put away his notebook. "And just why are you here? I don't remember inviting you."

Franks paused to brush off his mac and set his feet apart the way he was taught in rhetoric class at Brooklyn Young Ladies Preparatory School (long story).

"To solve the case!" he announced, "using modern technological methods." He approached the body.

"Right," Grimes huffed. "With your—what do you call it again?"

"Homoscience. I–do I hear sniggering?"

He glanced at the two cops, who were trying in vain to suppress their giggles. Undeterred, the doctor continued.

"It's a new field I'm pioneering: applying scientific principles to the solving of homicide cases. Ergo, I am a homoscientist."

The cops hugged themselves and emitting girlish titters. Franks was fairly certain one of them had said *wooo, wooo!* But he was used to their lowbrow humor, even when, ironically, it went over his head.

"So what does your, uh, homoscience tell you about this case?" Grimes asked, and to his credit almost didn't smirk.

Franks leaned against one of the supply shelves that covered the walls, his back to the others. "You're the detective, Grimes. What do you make of it?"

"First, stop sniffing the mimeograph fluid. Second, my preliminary guess would be accident. The machine was on a shelf and fell as the victim was trying to pull it down."

"Please. No one keeps a mimeograph machine on an upper shelf," the doctor scoffed, pausing to dab a bit of fluid behind each ear before returning the bottle to the counter. "Besides, these shelves are full."

"Suicide, then."

4

"No, no, no. Mr. Mishnik, being all of 120 pounds, could not have had the strength to lift this machine himself." He turned away from the group again, partly as a snub but mostly to pilfer a few gum erasers on a middle shelf.

"Which means someone in the office dropped it on him," Grimes said.

The doctor laughed and coughed up some phlegm. He had slept in due to a late-night Scrabble tournament and had not yet had the chance to clear his lungs with a healthy morning cigarette. Instinctively he pulled out one of his signature brand, a Turkish Dandy.

Inspector Grimes eyed him with suspicion.

"Grimes, are you proposing that the dainty Miss Chanelle hoisted the mimeograph machine over her head and crushed Mr. Mishnik in a fit of rage?"

Grimes rolled his eyes. "I asked what you thought, doctor," he said at last.

Dr. Franks bent down over the mimeograph machine and carefully extracted a pencil from the exposed inside breast pocket of the victim's herringbone jacket. "I believe it was murder."

"Oh for the love of–" Grimes said. "You just said no one in this office could do it."

Dr. Franks ran the pencil under his nose and cocked an eyebrow. "No. No one in this office."

They were interrupted by the sound of tires screeching outside, followed by a dull thump. Grimes crossed to the window and gazed down.

"It's just Sergeant Dingle," he said after a moment. "Hit by a taxi again. Now, where were we?"

"I was saying that this death may look like an accident, but is, in fact–" the great man paused for effect. "The latest in a mysterious series of strange and related deaths."

Inspector Grimes sighed heavily. "Okay boys–I think we're done here.

Dr. Franks cut them off at the door. "I believe," he said quickly, "this case is related to two other recent homicides."

Grimes put on his weather-beaten hat. "You've got twenty seconds."

"Fact: one week ago a scrawny proofreader at Encyclopedia Britannica was found dead under a three-volume set of the Oxford English Dictionary. Fact: a fortnight ago the ectomorphic choir director at St. Andrew's was crushed by the weight of his own massive organ. I believe–there's that sniggering again."

"I'm sorry," Grimes said as he exchanged raised eyebrows with the uniformed officers. "Did you say 'crushed by his own massive organ?'" This produced another fit of giggling. After composing himself, Grimes wiped tears from his eyes and said, "But what makes you think these cases are related?"

"All three victims were smallish. All were alone. All were crushed by objects obviously too heavy for them to have lifted."

"Meaning?" Grimes growled.

Dr. Franks slipped the pencil into an envelope, which he tucked away in his overcoat.

"To ascertain that, I have but to examine this item, along with some personal effects from the other victims, and test them for chemical substances and other commonalities. In other words, expose them to the rigors of my virgin homoscience."

"Wooo, wooo!" an officer blurted.

"Oh grow up!" Dr. Franks said. "Now, can any of you light my faggot? Oh really! What did I say now?"

THE BASEMENT

Phhhhttt!

The fluorescent lights flickered briefly before going out. A man muttered a mild expletive and slowly extracted himself from his ancient office chair. It was late morning and there was enough daylight pushing through the basement window to allow him to find his way to the fuse box. He reached into a crumpled brown paper bag on a nearby metal shelf and, with a practiced hand, swapped out bad fuse for good. The lights blinked on, revealing for an eighth of a second a seemingly random collection of dismantled machinery and scattered laboratory equipment before there was another *phhhffft!* and relative darkness again filled the room.

A woman's voice called down from upstairs: "Try unplugging it this time, genius!"

"I know, mother!"

Dr. Franks approached a lidded metal trash can and gave it a gentle kick. The large wad of aluminum foil that had been holding it open fell inside and the lid shut with a whump. He sat back down and sighed. Another setback.

On any given day, his mother's basement was the doctor's favorite place in the world. For one thing it was where he kept all his chemicals and power tools. It also housed his large and eclectic library of text books on subjects ranging from ventriloquism to relativity theory. He spent many humid summer nights in the cool subterranean lair, sketching plans for inventions and reading from his collection of Little Lulu comic books. Often he would fall asleep on the old truck seat in the corner, which was more comfortable than his lumpy mattress upstairs.

But today Dr. Franks was unhappy. And as usual his unhappiness stemmed from a severe lack of funds. The balance in his account at the Greenwich Village Uptown Bank & Feed had become so low he wasn't even allowed to take pieces of hard candy from the teller's window unless he was making a cash deposit. And now the blood bank was limiting him to one plasma donation per week. He needed to come up with another lucrative invention, and fast.

Above his desk was a large advertising poster: a smiling housewife balancing a dainty finger on a pale green countertop appliance with a caption above her reading, *I have more time for vacuuming now that I own a Federal Electric Can Opener!* The invention had been a commercial success, had in fact been the only of his numerous creations to make any money at all. Sadly, the royalties were slow in arriving and his accountant, Cousin Phelps, was at a loss to explain why. Or, more accurately, was never around to explain why.

The odd thing about the electric can opener was that Dr. Franks never thought it would catch on. Who, after all, would purchase a large, expensive electric product when the compact manual version worked just as well?

Everyone, as it turned out.

Dr. Franks waggled his finger accusingly at the housewife in the poster. "Electricity—that's the draw," he told her. "People are enamored with electricity."

This consumer desire for plug-in gizmos had been the inspiration for his recent series of experiments. The problem was he was running out of things to electrify. The other members of the 28th Street Inventors Society had taken all the good ideas: electric tie racks, battery-operated novelty coin banks and the like. The ideas Dr. Franks was developing–both AC and DC–left something to be desired. The electric shoes worked, of course, but also emitted an annoying buzzing sound that angered cats. (Perhaps, he mused, he could market a buzzing pet fence made of two-inch pumps). The electrified reclining chair seemed promising until the vibrations loosened the wiring and sent a current through the occupant (he had made a mental note to pitch it to the department of corrections as a humane method of capital punishment).

With this latest device–the hands-free trash can–he thought he was onto something. A mere tap with one's shoe caused the lid to open. No fuss, no muss. In retrospect, though, he should have added some insulation. A tin can or paper clip often shorted the thing out. But insulation would add to production costs.

Yet he had to make money somehow.

He stared vacantly at a haphazard pile of blue litmus paper. Perhaps, he thought, I should skip electricity and move on to atomics. He made another mental note to see about getting his hands on some cake uranium.

Dr. Franks considered himself a renaissance man, though jack-of-all-trades might have been nearer the mark. His fertile mind produced a bumper crop of ideas; the trick was making one or two of them profitable. Homoscience, for one. He had assisted Inspector Grimes on a few cases, but only on a pro bono basis, the Dagger of Damascus (the maid did it) and the Unlocked Room of Death with Several Windows (the maid did *not* do it). In both cases the doctor had solved them so quickly there wasn't time to seek remuneration. That was why, in this case, he was jumping in before he was even certain there was a homicide to solve. Good homoscience solved a crime; profitable homoscience produced billable hours.

As he sat pondering his financial woes, the basement window above the work bench opened with a creak. A large and lumpy squirrel leaned cautiously into the room, reaching for a yellow melamine bowl on the top shelf.

"That's right, Dash. Come and get your num nums."

The squirrel started at the voice and backed out. Dr. Franks clicked his tongue encouragingly. Dash pushed his head and front legs back into the room, just far enough to reach the bowl. Dr. Franks nodded in approval. It had only been a few months since he had started leaving out bowls of Trix for the skinny rodent; now the creature was twenty pounds if it was an ounce. As a modern scientist, Dr. Franks knew processed foods were more nutritious than natural foods like acorns and nuts. Tastier too.

Dash stuffed his cheeks with breakfast cereal and then wiggled his bulky gray body back outside and waddled off. The doctor turned his attention back to the electric recliner. After swapping out a few resistors, he plugged it in. At first, it seemed to work as expected, vibrating softly and giving off a bit of warmth. Then the upholstery caught fire and he had to fetch the fire extinguisher.

As he put out the last of the flames, the door at the top of the stairs opened slightly, sending a sliver of light across the work bench.

"Bernie," his mother called, "are you all right?"

Dr. Franks folded his arms and looked straight ahead.

"Yes, mother."

"No need to call the ambulance like last time?"

"No, mother."

He waited. Here it comes, he thought.

"Oh—while I'm here, can I ask you to put away your toys? I need the parlor today."

"They're not toys!"

"It says Tinker Toys right on the box."

"I happen to be creating a representation of a complex carbon molecule."

"Well, whatever. Can you put them away? I'm hosting bridge club this afternoon."

"As soon as I invent something."

The next hour was spent tinkering, but to no avail. He tootled on his slide whistle, an exercise that tended to occupy his reptilian brain while leaving the higher thought centers free to innovate. But a half hour of jazz scales produced nothing except a loud pounding on the floor above him.

"I've simply got to get my own place," Dr. Franks told his acid rack. Yet he knew that was unlikely in his current financial condition. He regretted, not for the last time, dropping out of Oxford. Or had it been Cambridge?

His musings were interrupted by the cacophonous sound of the upstairs doorbell. Some months prior he had whacked it with a tennis racquet while trying to invent an indoor version of the sport (he had never heard of racquetball) and ever since the bell produced a series of four muted, off-key notes that could best be described as a xylophone with a head cold.

Dr. Franks was about to call for his mother to attend to the visitor; however the creaking of the floorboards told him she was already on the case. How could a 90-pound woman have such heavy footfalls? He heard the door open and, after a beat, her voice ringing out clearly, even with the floor between them:

"Jesus Christ–what the hell do you want?"

There was a muffled reply. A man's voice.

"He's downstairs. Doing god knows what. Bernie!!"

Dr. Franks took a breath and held it. He really needed to get his own place.

The basement door opened and the man stomped purposefully down the stairs. On his head was a hat that had once been black, in his mouth a shredded object that had once been a cigar.

"Franks."

"Inspector Grimes."

The detective was a man of few words. Not that he wasn't talkative—he just had a severely limited vocabulary. Reading one of his police reports was like perusing a Dick and Jane Reader.

Grimes looked around suspiciously. Then, seeing a chair covered with a tarp, made a move toward it.

"Wait!" Dr. Franks rushed over and stopped him. "Let me make sure it's unplugged."

Seeing the electric cord dangling from the side, Grimes sat down with more care than he was used to. He put his crumpled hat top down on his lap and placed his cigar butt inside for safe keeping. Dr. Franks went back to his office chair. Grimes surveyed the room as if it were a crime scene.

"Your mother asked that you clean up your, uh, atom."

"It's a molecule."

As if on cue, they heard the hum of the vacuum cleaner upstairs.

"I was just having some lemonade, Inspector Grimes. Would you care for a glass?"

Grimes nodded, but his eyes were on a noisy assemblage of bubbling beakers and steaming tubes in the opposite corner. He turned back in time to see the doctor pour a white powder from his chemistry set into a large beaker. Franks then poured the mixture into two glasses, added a few cubes of ice from a bucket, and handed one glass to Grimes.

"What the blazes—?"

"Of all the chemicals in my new Ace-Descent 201-Piece Deluxe Chemistry Set," Dr. Franks said, "I like citric acid the best. Magnesium can be fun too, but it makes a horrible beverage. Cheers!"

The doctor took a hearty swig from his glass. Grimes took a quick sip and nodded his approval.

"I'm here to ask your help," he said, setting the glass on the dismantled air conditioner beside him.

Dr. Franks leaned back, pressing his fingers together thoughtfully. A chair spring popped. "You have come to seek my expertise as a..." He paused.

"Oh, don't make me say it!"

"Because I'm a..."

"All right. Because you're a homoscientist. Honestly, you've got to work on that name." He grabbed his beaker and took another swig. "Hey. This stuff ain't half bad."

Mother Franks gave the door several vigorous raps with the vacuum. They waited until the assault abated.

"I knew you'd come to appreciate the value of my fledgling discipline. After all, didn't I prove that the Jenkins suicide was actually a murder made to look like a suicide by the brother-in-law hanging upside down in the victim's closet when he fired the fatal shot?"

Grimes looked at the floor. "Uh, yeah."

"And wasn't it me who determined that the man found hung in that locked room with no furniture had taken a running leap to get his head through that noose?"

"Right." Grimes shifted uncomfortably. "Actually, there was another reason. There's been another, um, suspicious death. You know Jimmy and Jacky?"

Dr. Franks nodded. Everyone knew the old vaudeville team. Jimmy played the big bully and Jacky the diminutive, droopy-eyed second banana.

"We just found Jacky dead backstage at the Comedy Cavalcade."

"Let me guess: under Jimmy."

"Bingo."

Dr. Franks leaned back and nodded thoughtfully. Another spring popped.

"So. When can you start?"

Profitability! The doctor smiled. "Perhaps we should discuss remuneration."

"We can't offer you much in terms of money—"

"My fee is twenty dollars a day."

"I'll give you ten a day and anything you can find in the squad refrigerator."

Dr. Franks suppressed a grin. He lived to haggle.

"What if I told you I had already made progress on the case? Would that be worth another $5 a day?"

Grimes, who had already risen to leave, had even donned his chapeau and clamped his incisors on his battered cigar, eyed Dr. Franks suspiciously.

"What do you mean?"

The doctor pitched himself up and bounded with surprising lightness toward the rattling beakers on the far side of the basement.

"Formic acid," he announced, holding up a Florence flask.

Inspector Grimes waited.

"Formic acid. I distilled it from the pencil in Mr. Mishnick's pocket."

"Just get to the point, will ya—hey, that's acid!"

Grimes' alarm was caused by Dr. Franks taking a sip from the flask.

"Relax. Folic acid is a harmless substance. It's found in apples."

"Formic acid."

Dr. Franks jerked his head. "What did I just say?"

"You said folic acid was found in apples. But you meant formic acid, right?"

"What happened now?" Dr. Franks asked when he came to. He was stretched out on the rickety bench against the back wall of the basement.

"You passed out," Grimes told him, a hint of suspicion in his voice. "The formic acid, remember?"

Dr. Franks sat up. His tongue tingled. "Right. Must make a mental note to keep my acids straight."

"Well, formic, folic, whatever—what does this have to do with anything?"

Dr. Franks dabbed his tongue with his hanky. "Well—it's something."

Inspector Grimes frowned.

"There were also traces of amphetamines, a form of hallucinogen and a hint of cinnamon." The doctor blinked. "Wow. I think I can actually see flavors."

Inspector Grimes walked noisily up the stairs and opened the door, pausing to poke his head back down. "Ten dollars a day—and no refrigerator privileges."

WANG'S CAJUN DELI

Although he had spent much of his youth abroad, Dr. Franks considered himself a New Yorker, and he knew the Island of Manhattan like a chef knows his onions. From the Bowery in the north to Harlem in the south, there was nary a side street or alley he hadn't wandered down or, all too often, woken up in. Not that the doctor was an imbiber; he merely suffered from narcolepsy.

Winters in New York were tolerable. Not as mild as Oxford or Cambridge where he spent his undergraduate years, but neither as frigid as Queen Elizabeth Island where he had joined his father's expedition in a long and fruitless search for the bones of the woolly unicorn. Spring was non-existent most years. Summers were survivable. But fall was when the city came alive. The crisp, clear air. The color of the leaves in Central Park made brilliant by the low sun. The general lack of underarm perspiration. All these contributed to the doctor's seasonal joie de vivre.

This fall morning was no different, for it was bright and calm and fairly warm if one stayed on the north or west side of the street to catch the sun. The midtown office buildings loomed above him like uneven molars in the mouth of a cyclopean Englishman. Limousines and pedestrians zoomed past in a friendly whirr of activity.

The corners of Dr. Franks' mouth turned up in a subtle smile. Under different circumstances these same sights and sounds would disturb him. But the autumnal light and the promise of a daily stipend had done much to brighten his mood. Things had worked out well, considering. Ten bucks a day! Frankly, he pulled that murder idea out of his pear-shaped buttocks. There was no evidence of a motive or a murderer, just an odd set of coincidences. But now this fourth incident with Jimmy and Jacky–maybe there was a genuine case here after all.

He turned up 20th St. and walked north along the East River. The water was deceptively calm with nary a corpse to mar its brown green surface. Even the abusive cursing of the Teamsters on the docks below seemed cheerful.

Dr. Franks continued on, staying in the sun when he could. The river brought with it a slight breeze that unfurled his raincoat and, he hoped, aired it out a bit in the bargain. He gave his cardigan a good shake to dislodge any stray crumbs or chemical compounds.

Finding himself on West 35th St. the doctor turned north onto a block of stately brownstones. A black sedan raced up and jerked to a halt a few yards ahead. The melancholy yet blessedly fleeting image of his own car came to his mind; a lovely 1952 Ford Crown Vic that had been purchased new from Dinky Dave Ford and had blown a rod not three months later.

His reverie was dissipated by a dapper man jumping out of the driver's side and dashing around to open the rear passenger door. Immediately a huge man in heavy overcoat and beaver skin hat emerged from the brownstone. He glanced nervously in both directions before marching with surprising grace toward the waiting car.

"Beautiful day, sir!" Dr. Franks said.

The large man—Franks guessed he weighed a seventh of a ton—raised his eyebrow a seventh of an inch and said, "Pfui." Seconds later, the sedan was gone and the street was quiet save for the rustling of leaves across the pavement.

Passing the Natural History Museum, the doctor noticed a short Japanese man in a three-piece suit. His diminutive stature put Dr. Franks' mind back on his homoscientific case. For four small men to die under such similar circumstances was certainly beyond coincidence. It would take him a while to piece it together, which was just as well as it meant the job, and the stipend, could be extended indefinitely. His new income stream, combined with the overdue can opener royalties, might be enough to finance a move to his own apartment. As much as he loved his mother's basement, it was time to get out on his own. Perhaps then he could make some time with the ladies. Miss Chanelle of Excelsior Bowling Apparel Co. Ltd. came to mind. And there was that buxom librarian he'd had his eye on...

Before he knew it he had arrived at his morning destination. He checked his fly and prepared to enter.

There is no place in the world like an authentic New York delicatessen and Wang's Cajun Deli was not that place. In fact, it was hard to say from a glance what manner of restaurant it was, or even that it was a restaurant at all. The sign above the storefront bore several conflicting words and logos. From left to right, a snooty waiter with a pencil-thin moustache and a towel draped over one forearm, a dancing neon crustacean (possibly a shrimp), a line drawing of a teapot emblazoned with the words "Chop Suey" and a yellow square bearing the text "Free Eye Exam."

Nor did the plate glass window offer much of a clue as to the cuisine, filled as it was with several commercial messages, all in neon: A hanger with the words "suits pressed while you wait" next to "corned beef pastrami" followed by "we never close" (just over a hand painted sign reading "CLOSED 4 P.M.") and "fine cigars."

These adornments, however, were dwarfed by an orange neon monstrosity depicting a large set of eyeglasses, with pupils that moved from left to right and back again.

Once inside one could guess, from the aroma if nothing else, that Wang's Cajun Deli was some type of eatery, and a busy one at that. Exactly what type of food it served would not be clear until one looked at one of the large, plastic-covered menus. A line of ten tables flanked the plate glass windows. In order: three melamines on shaky pedestal bases, six booths with worn vinyl benches and, in the corner, a round, table paired with two tall yet mismatched stools. Three weathered high-backed wooden booths (survivors of the establishment's bauhaus period) formed the base of the L. The requisite counter ran parallel to the windows, its surface weathered with age, coffee and the skin oil of six decades of diners. Close inspection revealed the counter had at some point been painted over with coarse ceiling paint. Close inspection, however, was not a habit of the cabbies, numbers runners and starving actresses who made up the breakfast and lunch crowd. Wang's Chinese Deli was closed for dinner.

In truth, the establishment had been many things in its long history, most of which could be guessed at and some (like a speakeasy and whorehouse) only rumored. But for the past thirty years it had always been one kind of restaurant or another. An anonymous wag had given it the name Wang's Cajun Deli (even though gumbo and crawfish had never been on the menu) and the name stuck.

It was located at a busy intersection in Midtown Manhattan, conveniently located near City Hall, Central Park, Harlem, the Battery and the Theater District.

Outside of his mother's basement, Wang's Chinese Deli was Dr. Franks' favorite place on earth. The food was cheap and never underdone. The clientele minded its own business.

The proprietor, a surly dark-haired Lebanese man named Gus, provided begrudgingly adequate service. And his penchant for punctuating his daily rants about the general unfairness of the world with jabs of a meat cleaver had long ago persuaded annoyingly chatty diners to take their business elsewhere.

As Dr. Franks entered he was met with the terrific aural blast–of a shouting match. Without flinching, he strolled back to his regular booth–the wooden one in the corner under a faded mural of the Grand Canal. There was no fight, merely the aforementioned Gus.

"This Nique-zone, he's trouble. Eisenhower will drop him like hot tomato."

Gus was facing the grill, his back to the counter, corralling an order of scrambled eggs and gesturing with his free arm and both shoulders.

"Nique-zone. He is crazy. And what is this with his dog?"

Gus deftly served up the eggs and held the plate to the kitchen window so the ancient cook on the other side could add the bacon and toast. Then Gus literally slammed the plate down on the counter in front of a dozing cop, who instinctively reached for his revolver. Gus paid him no heed, but continued his speech to the delivery driver at the end of the counter.

"I'll tell you about dogs," Gus screamed casually, jabbing his spatula (the cleaver apparently having taken the morning off). "They are filthy. Worse than pigs. At least pigs you can eat. More bacon!" This last he called back to the kitchen. The ancient cook, a relative of Gus's whom the doctor had nicknamed Uncle Tonoose, responded by turning up the radio. Gus, in turn, increased his own volume.

Dr. Franks smiled warmly as he took in the scene. The breakfast crowd, even Gus's intended audience, completely ignored the tirade. They were regulars. Gus was in mid-season form. He had strong Mediterranean features, highlighted by a large, handsome nose. The hair poked out from under his paper hat like Canadian thistle. The doctor held up his cup and waved it. Gus, seeing the gesture out of the corner of his eye, nodded quickly but continued his lecture.

"Pigs are wonderful creatures. Smarter than dogs. And meatier. More decaf!"

While Uncle Tonoose appeared with a full carafe of Sanka, Gus hurried over to Dr. Franks' table and splashed regular into and around his cup.

"The usual, my friend?"

"Corned beef, no pickle." The doctor mopped up the spill with a paper napkin. "I'm eating light this morning."

Gus sped down the aisle, sprinkling coffee in a random fashion. No one seemed offended, except a delivery man who was obviously a newcomer.

Dr. Franks took the morning papers out of his coat pocket and dumped them on the bench beside him. From his A&P bag (the good kind with the twine handles) he produced a weathered brown notebook and opened it to the first blank page. Ten minutes later he had filled three pages with notes, cleaned his plate and left greasy fingerprints on virtually every section of every paper.

The doctor's first of many unwritten rules of homoscience that he was making up as he went along was that nothing was out of bounds, especially when charging by the day. Therefore, he began this case with a thorough perusing of the dailies. Also, he was intrigued by Smokey Stover. More often than one would guess he found some article of interest. From the *Herald* he extracted the name and address of the editor's widow. In the *Sun* he noted the deceased choir director had no next of kin. From the *Times* he tore out a coupon for athletic socks. The other two deaths had not made the early editions.

He finished his last sip of coffee, turned the cup upside down and reviewed his notes. The handwriting was frenetic and uneven. To a stranger, and sometimes the doctor, it was indecipherable. Still, he was satisfied with the morning's work.

On the final page was a list of totals, an estimate of his current net worth. It was a woefully low number, especially after subtracting the breakfast tab. He had hoped to run into Cousin Phelps at Wang's so he could ask about his royalties, but the man was nowhere to be seen.

"My friend, for a hundred dollars I sell this place and move back to the old country."

Gus cleared away the plates.

"You've been saying that ever since you bought the place in '46."

"Aaaa," Gus spat, waving the dishware around to make his point. "Anything good in the papers?"

Dr. Franks held up the coupon.

"Sweat socks."

Gus shifted the dishes into one arm so he could rub a thumb and forefinger together.

"You must have a case, eh, Mr. Bags of Money?"

The doctor nodded.

Gus leaned forward and said confidentially, but still loudly enough for the pots and pans man to hear without difficulty, "I know who did it."

Dr. Franks frowned and braced himself. "Who?" he asked reluctantly.

"The butler!" Gus cried. It was an old joke the restaurateur never tired of. He danced away, laughing like a mental patient. No one looked up.

THE 14TH PRECINCT

Dr. Franks paid his bill and stuffed his materials into his A&P bag (the good kind with the twine handles).

For billing purposes, if nothing else, it behooved him to make an appearance at the Homicide Division. Yesterday's visit from Inspector Grimes made that day count as a work day, and a few hours spent looking at police reports would round off this one. Dr. Franks did not believe in charging by the hour; to his way of thinking, he was always on the case.

He walked eleven blocks to the 14th Precinct at 12nd and 31st, home of Inspector Grimes' Homicide Division. Yankee Stadium was empty but there were plenty of tourists around the Empire State Building. Dr. Franks had tried to catch a taxi, but the driver recognized him and swerved away from the curb at the last minute. The cabbies seemed to be avoiding him, despite the wealth of useful driving advice he generously provided them from the back seat.

Upon entering the homicide unit, he made a bee-line for the freezer and grabbed a banana Popsicle. No matter what Inspector Grimes said, he was establishing his refrigerator privileges. Then he strode confidently into the inspector's office.

Grimes was poring over some reports. The half-eaten tuna fish sandwich at his elbow had had ample time to act as a potpourri. The inspector looked up.

"Oh, yeah. You'll probably want to see the case files. They're in interrogation room one. I'm going over to interview Jimmy Fulch at the Cavalcade at four if you want to come along."

Grimes did a double take, eyeing Dr. Franks with suspicion. "Where did you get that?"

The doctor gave the Popsicle a long, dramatic lick. "You want me to put it back?"

The files were sparse—semiliterate, acronym-laden scribblings of nine-to-five detectives—and revealed little.

Lex Harrison, choir directer, St. Andrew's. 42. Bachelor. ID'd from dental (upper torso and extremeties crushed). TOD—10:22 pm (approx.) COD—piano accident. Next of kin—Rev. William Peeples (coworker).

The other two files were more of the same—short on information and long on inaccuracies (Piano indeed, Dr. Franks harrumphed).

Eric Sampson, sr. editer, Encycl. Britannia. 37. Married (Linda). TOD—4:30 pm (approx.) COD—book accident...

Jerome Mishnik, 35, accountant, Excelsior Bowling. TOD—5:15 pm. COD—crushed by copy machine. Next of kin—parents, Albert and Helen, Brooklyn...

The fourth case report, for Jacky Fulch of Jimmy and Jacky, was not yet available. Neither were the coroner's reports.

He went through the boxes of personal effects found on Sampson, Harrison and Mishnick. From the first he took the editor's pica stick, from the second the choir director's baton, and placed both items in his A&P bag.

There was not much else of interest. The editor's wallet had a Diners Club card, a rotary club membership card and a few business cards. Choir director Harrison's had less than that: no driver's license, two dollars and a membership card to something called the Societas Homoformicidae.

Homoformicidae.

Dr. Franks sniffed the card. Cinnamon. He went back to the editor's wallet. Sure enough, among the business cards was one for the same club: Societas Homoformicidae. Both cards bore only those words and the name of the cardholder. Plus an odd little icon: a vertical line with a dot at the top intersected by three shorter horizontal lines. A quick check revealed that Mishnick's wallet contained the same card.

The doctor walked out to the bathroom and washed the Popsicle syrup off his hands. When he returned to the interrogation room he carefully put the three membership cards in a baggy. His Latin was a bit rusty, but a trip to the library would remedy that.

It was a strange case, to be sure. Four small, meek men, all crushed to death in varying fashions, and at least three members of the same oddly-named club. He knew they were murders, all right. Unless, of course, they were suicides. Or accidents.

Determining the current time took a bit of ciphering since his wristwatch was set to Greenwich Mean Time, currently seven o'clock in the evening. That would make it 3 p.m. in New York—no, Daylight Saving Time had just ended, so it was 2 p.m. Eastern Time. They weren't going to interview Fulch until 4 p.m. He stuffed his materials into his A&P bag and headed for the door.

The library it was.

Outside of his mother's basement and Wang's Chinese Deli, Dr. Franks' favorite place in the whole world was the New York City Main Library. He loved its neoclassical architecture, reveled in the mildew-y aroma of ancient texts and appreciated the fact that they let him sleep there as long as his snoring didn't bother the other patrons. Perhaps it was these things, combined with his thirst for knowledge, that compelled him to return almost daily. Or it might have been the red hot dame at the circulation desk. He would watch her for hours, fascinated by her delicate bone structure, the healthy glow of her skin and a rear end reminiscent of two gravity-defying bowling balls. He knew everything about her. Cindy was her name. Or maybe Cathy. But she was more than a natural beauty, as he learned from numerous conversations.

"Hot enough for you?" Dr. Franks would quip as he handed her a request slip for *True Crime, National Geographic* or some other research journal. Or sometimes, "Heavy water has an extra oxygen atom that makes it unstable." And Cathy (Karen?) would be ready with some precocious reply like, "My eyes are up here buddy" or "Do you sleep in that raincoat?" Often Dr. Franks would request a specific issue of *Redbook* just so he could watch her wiggle her way all the way down the aisle directly behind her. He was a brilliant and lonely man.

Today, Carleen had her silky blonde hair pulled back and stacked on top of her perfectly rounded head in a twisted bun. The doctor appreciated this particular coif because it made Candice look like she was trying to look smart, which he found endearing. It also made him crave an apricot Danish. But the librarian look, intended or no, was offset by her ensemble: a form-fitted white angora sweater and even more form-fitting burnt orange skirt.

The overall effect, as she shimmied down the aisles to retrieve the requested periodicals, was enough to make a husband forget his wife, a priest forget his vows and a teenager forget to breathe. Dr. Franks' mind, however (at least part of it) was preoccupied with the case.

"You borrowed this *Redbook* last week."

Caitlyn had returned, her full lips compressed into a fetching pout.

"I, um, need to copy a Jell-o recipe for my mother."

She gave him a sidelong glance. He smiled weakly.

"Also, the new issue of the *JPSR* hasn't come in yet. You want the old one?"

"Quel dommage."

"Who?"

Dr. Franks sighed. "That is a yes."

She handed him his stack of magazines. He took them and then paused.

"May I add that that is a fetching sweater?"

Katherine exhaled loudly and looked toward the ceiling. "I wish you wouldn't."

Dr. Franks sat down at his usual table, in a small nook flanked by children's encyclopediae and Nassau County case law, tossed aside the *Redbook* and studied the cover of the *JPSR*, or *Journal of Pseudo-scientific Research*. A black-and-white illustration depicted a noseless, earless humanoid seen through the transparent dome of a flying disc; in one hand the figure held a steering wheel, in the other an empty bottle. Its oversized head sagged to one side and it had two X's for eyes. The headline above it read: ROSWELL UFO CRASH: DRUNKEN ALIEN TO BLAME? He had already read this issue, of course, but it never hurt to give the periodical a second go-through.

The doctor held the *JPSR* in high esteem, to the point of considering a subscription. But then he'd have one fewer reason to visit the circulation desk. The *JPSR*, more so than the respectable journals, kept Dr. Franks up on the cutting edge of science. Franks noticed that scientific pioneers throughout history were initially condemned as frauds before being welcomed (often posthumously) into the fraternity of academic orthodoxy. Galileo, Pasteur and Einstein had all been labeled crackpots in their day, as had Dr. Franks himself—and nobody covered the crackpots like the *JPSR*. The fact that real crackpots were also initially considered crackpots did not tarnish his respect for the publication. So what if most of the stories were a bit dubious? It was still a better read than *Scientific American.*

He paged through the periodical. Pretty much the same old stuff: a grainy photo of an little green man who looked suspiciously like a lemur, an account of javelin-shaped fish perforating Amazonian fishermen, an interview with a Minnesota farmer who had been kidnapped by Venusians and subsequently taken to wearing aluminum foil overalls.

He was engrossed in a story about an Artic expedition that hoped to prove Euler's hollow earth theory (they had lost their way somewhere near Banff) when, for no particular reason, he gazed over at *World Book Children's Encyclopedia, Vol. 3, (Cannibalism to Cthulhu).* His brain itched slightly, as if he were forgetting something. Had he come here with a specific task? Suddenly it came to him.

Latin!

He looked at his watch: 7:30. Minus four meant 3:30 Eastern. I should have just enough time, he thought.

BACKSTAGE

Dr. Franks gave the homicide division coffee pot a sideways glance. The liquid was soupy and black. A greasy blue haze rose from the carafe. It looked delicious. The time was 3:50 (8:50 GMT) and Inspector Grimes was reaching for his coat. Just enough time to pour a cup and add his customary eight cubes of sugar. He took a few quick slurps. Oily, bitter, with that salty hint of burnt grounds. Bracing. Still...

"Where did you get that?" Inspector Grimes asked, eyeing the doctor with suspicion.

They were in a squad car, heading for the Comedy Cavalcade on the upper Northwest side. Inspector Grimes was in the passenger seat. Dr. Franks was directly behind him, trying to stay out of his line of sight.

"Is that the other half of my tuna sandwich? Jesus, Franks!"

"I was famished. I've not eaten in four hours."

Outside, the sun was low and the wind had picked up. Pedestrians were leaning into the gusts, collars upturned.

Inspector Grimes chewed another half inch off his cigar. "Now when we get there let me do the talking. The last thing I want is for the scandal sheets to get the idea that we're investigating some kind of crazy midget murder spree."

Dr. Franks licked his fingers. "I like the sound of that: Midget Murder Spree."

"No, no, no! There are some odd coincidences here: the manner of death, the size of the victims. That's why you're here. But as far as the police are concerned, as far as I'm concerned, these are still four unrelated deaths."

The doctor watched Grimes' bald head jerk angrily from side to side. It was wide and pale and reminded him of a porcelain toaster.

"As long as I get my fifteen bucks a day."

"I thought we said ten."

"Let's just make it thirteen then."

Jerry and Jacky Fulch had been, up to Jacky's untimely demise, a famous and beloved duo. They started in the vaudeville circuit as The Funny Fulch Brothers and their act had included a bit of everything: soft shoe, grifting, slapstick. Especially slapstick. Onstage, Jerry was the smarter, bigger, abusive brother and Jacky the stupider, shorter, abused sibling. Nearly every bit would end with Jacky being smacked on top of the head, falling to his knees and uttering his famous line, "Check please!"

Offstage, things were pretty much the same.

They made a series of successful movies for Twentieth Century Fox, including *Hobo Hijinks, The Mistaken Millionaire* and *Jerry & Jacky Join the Seabees* (also known as *Propellers Aweigh*).

In the Fifties there was little use for the duo at the studios, where lavish big screen pageantry was in vogue. Even feigning communist sympathies got them no press. Neither could they find a place on television, since Milton Berle had cornered the market on dull-witted humor. So they were back to doing stage shows, usually as an opening act for bigger, younger names like Eddie Fisher and Chatter.

Dr. Franks and Grimes found Jimmy in his backstage dressing room, sitting on a chair, wearing a ruffled shirt, black socks and little else. His pants and underwear were hanging from a valet nearby ("to prevent wrinkling," he explained). There was nothing memorable about his face, save that it was wrinkled, puffy and famous.

"Mr. Fulch, I'm Inspector Grimes of the NYPD. We're sorry about your loss—"

"Sir, can you perhaps put on some trousers?"

"And this is Dr. Franks."

"A homo—"

"He's a consultant."

Fulch looked up. The bloodshot eyes and red nose told Dr. Franks that the man had been crying or drinking or both. Fulch went into the bathroom and returned a moment later wearing a towel that barely circumnavigated his waist.

"I just have some routine questions about the accident," Grimes said. He shot a preemptive glance at Dr. Franks upon uttering the word accident. For once, the doctor got the message and kept his mouth shut.

Fulch crossed to a dresser, his back to the visitors. He was looking at a framed photo, a movie still. The brothers were dressed as clowns and Jimmy was about to clobber Jacky with an oversized mallet.

"That was from *Lyin' Tamers*," he said as if to himself. "After Jacky recovered from his concussion he said that was the best bit we ever filmed. He was a comic genius. The way he'd lose consciousness—you just can't teach that."

Inspector Grimes coughed. "From what I understand, you and your brother had an altercation?"

Fulch turned. "We were just goofing around, the way brothers do. You know, a little punch to the head, a friendly eye gouge."

"And then you fell on him?"

Fulch buried his face in his hands. "Oh, God. He was so tiny, you know? And I've—I've put on a few pounds. It was horrible." He collapsed on the couch. The towel strained ominously.

"Perhaps you'd feel better if you got dressed," Dr. Franks volunteered.

Inspector Grimes eyed Fulch suspiciously. From the neck up.

"I don't get it." He had his notebook out and was tapping it with his pencil. "You just—fell on him and he died?"

Fulch raised his head and looked straight at the inspector. The tears in his eyes seemed genuine. "I didn't exactly fall on him. He tried to pick me up."

Grimes tilted his head. "Pick you up? Pick you *up?*" He jotted something down and then looked back at the beefy entertainer. "Pick *you* up?"

"I'm afraid we were having an argument. About a girl. A dancer here. I can get her name for you if you want. It was silly. I mean, sure I stole her from Jacky, but I always do that. No big deal. I'm the big brother—"

"Obviously," Dr. Franks said, carefully examining the ceiling. "Now about those pants."

Grimes held a hand up to the doctor. Fulch continued.

"Last night Jacky tells me he's tired of being the little guy. But what can I do about it? I'm six-two, he is—was—five-four. Anyway, he says from now on he's going to be in charge. He's going to be the strong one. He said—" he paused. "Well, it's crazy."

Grimes finished scribbling, then said, "Go on. What did he say?"

"Jacky said, he said he could pick me up over his head. He wouldn't let up about it. So—so I let him try. And he couldn't, of course. And blammo—I fell on him and broke his neck. Oh, God!"

Grimes shook his head. Bits of tobacco flew from his unlit stogie. "Why would he say that?"

"He had been talking like that for weeks. I think he was working out. Some kind of mail order thing, I guess. Positive thinking and weight lifting. I don't know." He buried his chin in his chest. "I'm sorry. Can we do this later?" He stood up. "It's just a horrible time for me right now."

"I don't think we have any more questions," Grimes said, putting away his notebook.

"I do," Dr. Franks said suddenly. He had been, for reasons of modesty, inspecting the dresser. "Is this yours?" He held up a business card by the edges. It featured a long line ending in a dot and intersected by three shorter lines.

Jimmy squinted at it. "Soc-si-a-teez-homo-form—what the hell? Oh—that was that crazy club Jacky joined. The one that put those crazy ideas in his head."

"You don't mind if I take it as evidence, then? Along with this club sandwich and pickle spear?"

"Whatever. Whatever. Just please leave me. I'm mourning a loss here." He raised his hands up as if in supplication. "Oh Jacky, if only I could clobber you one more time."

Grimes grabbed Dr. Franks and pushed him forcefully toward the door.

Fulch addressed the doctor. "By the way, what's with the phony English accent?"

Dr. Franks bristled. "I'll have you know I studied at Oxford. And/or Cambridge."

It was dark as they rode back to the precinct.

"The business card I get," Grimes said, "but why the sandwich?"

"Still hungry."

THE EVIDENCE

Day Three of the Murder Midget Spree was a busy one. To save time, the doctor breakfasted at home. The Franks family rarely talked at the table, but this particular morning the silence was what only could be termed awkward.

"You didn't have to throw it in the backyard," Dr. Franks muttered at last.

Mama Franks sat opposite her son, the small formica table between them strewn with disassembled morning newspapers, plates, spoons, condiments and a plastic St. Christopher figurine with a glop of jelly on its haloed head.

His mother did not respond immediately, simply took a loud sip of her tea overloaded with milk. Finally, without looking up from the A&P ad she was studying she said evenly, "I asked you several times to move that atom."

"But I was really onto something. Possibly a carbon molecule with a smaller and more stable structure. Do you know what that would mean?" He gestured with his butter knife, sending marmalade on a looping arc toward the business section.

"That you'd drag more Tinker Toys into the house? I told you I was taking company yesterday. I couldn't just leave the thing. There would have been no room for the card table."

Dr. Franks gave up, watching silently as his mother's strong, deft hands carefully ripped out a coupon for Folger's coffee and laid it neatly on top of a growing stack: five cents off russet potatoes, two cans of StarKist for ten cents, a five-cent rebate for Brazzo. It was hard to imagine her as the bold young woman who was more than a match for his famous father. In her day, Mama Franks had been a suffragette and aviator. Now her biggest adventure was "taking company," as she called it. The doctor was pretty sure she got the phrase from watching *Gone with the Wind.*

After breakfast he put the remains of the molecule back in the living room and then spent time examining the evidence from the case: the pica stick, the baton, the pencil and, most importantly, the business cards. The club sandwich and pickle spear were long gone.

Societas Homoformicidae. All four victims had owned a card bearing that name and the curious pictogram. The phone book had no such listing, but according to the library's Latin dictionary, it loosely translated as *Society of the Antmen.* Ants, of course, were small yet strong—able to lift up to ten times their own weight. From what Jimmy Fulch had said, it was some kind of self-improvement program involving what had proved to be a deadly combination of positive thinking and weight-lifting. Was it possible, the doctor mused, that this Antman Society was the link between the cases? Assuming there was a case.

Dash made a quick appearance, reaching in through the basement window just long enough to stuff his cheeks with Coco Puffs. Dr. Franks heard the squirrel's labored wheezing from across the room and wondered if the creature had been overexerting itself. But at least, he concluded, it had a thick layer of fat for winter.

The doctor found no fingerprints on any of the items other than those of the respective victims. He did, however, have samples from the pieces of evidence on the boil and suspected they would show traces of the same compound as Mishnick's pencil; namely: formic acid and hallucinogens. And cinnamon. He hoped so, anyway.

Then he was off to Wang's for a quick pastrami sandwich. The day was overcast and windy, and the thick clouds churned like waves on a rough sea. The Flatiron Building looked like the prow of the *Titanic* just before it met the iceberg. It had rained that morning, and could do so again any minute. Dr. Franks held up his hand, but the taxis ignored him as usual. There was nothing to do but button up his putty overcoat and head into the wind.

"So my friend, did the butler do it?" Gus shouted cheerfully as Dr. Franks entered the restaurant.

The doctor said nothing, simply took a seat at the counter and turned his cup right-side up.

"No booth today? More soup!" Gus yelled.

"In a hurry."

"The library today? Sometimes I go there and look at the picture books of my beautiful homeland." He waved his cleaver joyfully.

"No. I'm working on a homicide case. As a paid consultant."

"Nice. You know my friend, for one hundred dollars American I would sell this place and move back. Do we have more banana cream!"

The doctor, feeling generous, left a dime tip for a fifty cent tab. He had managed to get his first two days' pay from Grimes (they had settled on $12 a day) so he felt he could afford it. It was never a bad idea to stay on the good side of a Lebanese man with a blade.

Outside, it was raining sideways. The drops were few, but cold and hard and hurt like Rasinettes hurled by an angry moviegoer (something of which the doctor had firsthand experience when, years earlier, he had pointed out the scientific inaccuracies of *Metropolis*). Dr. Franks shuffled sideways down Lexington until reaching the relative safety of the leeward side of the Flatiron Building. After that it was fairly easy to cut through Grand Central Station. He considered getting his Hush Puppies buffed, thought better of it, and exited onto East 73rd St. By then, both the wind and rain had slackened, and it was a mere two blocks to Einstein's newsstand.

Einstein was not his real name. Nobody knew Einstein's real name except his family, and nobody knew if he had family. Everybody called him Einstein due to his numerous similarities to the great mathematician. Einstein had the same unkempt thatch of wiry hair, bushy eyebrows, puppy dog eyes and fish lips as his namesake.

"Hey, doc. Did you watch *Lawrence Welk* last night? Great accordion duet with Myron Floren. Do you like Myron Floren? I think he's going to take over the show some day."

Everything except the genius part. Nevertheless, he was the doctor's best friend.

"Shut up, Einstein."

Einstein stepped out from under the awning of his weathered news hut and began making neat stacks of early and late editions.

"I won't be here in a few weeks. I'm going to Florida for vacation. How 'bout that?"

Dr. Franks took the papers and paid Einstein.

"I hear you're on a case. Do you need an assistant?"

"No."

"Remember I helped you that one time? The icehouse murder?"

Dr. Franks thumbed through the *Daily News*. "Yes."

"I'm always right here. Except for eleven to twelve, when I'm at lunch. And the first week of December, 'cause I'll be in Florida. How 'bout that?"

"Gotcha, I–" The doctor noticed an odd document wedged between the sports page and the classifieds. "Is this…a manuscript?"

"I typed up one of your cases," Einstein said. "Just like Doctor Watson for Sherlock Holmes. 'Cept of course you're the doctor."

"You can type?"

"Night school. I'm up to thirty words a minute. How 'bout that?"

Dr. Franks stuffed the papers in his A&P bag. "I'll take a look."

"You off to the library?"

"Actually, I'm off to interview witnesses."

"You need a bodyguard? I'd go with you except I have to run the newsstand. Except the first week in December–"

"Shut up, Einstein."

ON THE TOWN

Dr. Franks took the subway all the way downtown to the Upper East Side. Soon he was craning his neck to view the high-rise residence of Linda Sampson, widow of Eric Simpson, the recently-deceased senior editor at the *Encyclopedia Britannica*.

"Deliveries in back."

"Sir, I am here on official police business."

The doorman gave Dr. Franks, who was dripping wet, a dubious once-over and went back to reading the paper.

"All right," the doctor relented, "where's the freight elevator?"

On the twenty-third floor, Dr. Franks transferred to the guest elevator and continued up the penthouse. There, he was met by a rather burly and unkempt servant who wrestled away his raincoat and showed him into the parlor. Through the floor-to-ceiling windows, the doctor noticed the sun was just breaking through the clouds, revealing Central Park and, beyond that, Queens. The room was large and well-appointed with paintings, vases and hanging fabrics. It was a posh place and he said so.

"This is a posh place," he said.

"We do the best we can."

He turned. The widow Sampson had entered the room. She was pretty, superhumanly blonde and a bit overweight. Or it might have been the dress, a revealing composition of silken ribbons, black in hue (she was, after all, in mourning) and tightly yet seemingly haphazardly wrapped from mid-thigh up to mid-bosom. Horizontal rolls of pink flesh were popping out all over. Dr. Franks wondered how long the woman could hold her breath.

"Mrs. Sampson. Quite a lovely home, though if I may say, a bit rococo."

"No. It's all paid for," she said, betraying a Brooklyn accent. "Um, could you help me down the step? I'm a sort of tightly wound here."

Taking the doctor's hand, Mrs. Sampson stepped carefully down into the parlor, made as if to sit down on a settee, thought better of it and leaned against the wall. She tried to find a comfortable yet casual position and, finding that impossible, simply took a large and obviously much-needed gulp of air.

"I don't want to rush you, but I have a memorial service to attend," she said, smiling through a twinge of pain.

"I just have a few more questions. I know the police have already taken your statement. Er—I have to ask, did Mr. Sampson come from money?"

"Eric?" She tried to laugh. "He was a self-made man." She fingered the double strand of pearls around her neck, which clanked like marbles. "You may not believe it from the looks of things, but neither of us comes from old money."

But Dr. Franks had wandered away, and was now scrutinizing an abstract painting on the far wall, a seemingly random collection of squiggly lines and geometric shapes. He leaned in, tracing lines with his finger a half an inch from the canvas.

"Is this guy bothering you, Linda? I mean—Mrs. Sampson? You want me to toss him?"

It was the loutish servant. He was hopping from foot to foot, left hand massaging right fist as if preparing to use it.

"Of course not, Wally. Mr. Franks is just asking a few questions."

"I don't trust him," Wally brooded. "It's them googily eyes."

"Nonsense, Wally. He's just a bit cross-eyed is all."

"Wall-eyed, actually," the doctor added.

The explanation did not satisfy Wally. He remained just within the room.

"You can go now, Wally," Mrs. Sampson said harshly. "I'll call if I need you."

Dr. Franks moved to another wall, and was now studying a large, dark painting above the divan.

"Like it? I've been told it's a genuine Vermeer.

"Really! Your husband must have done very well in his job as an, um, editor."

"Senior editor."

Dr. Franks coughed. "Yes. Of course. Senior editor. I just ask because you seem to be fairly well endowed."

Mrs. Sampson's eyes flashed. Then she put her head down and added demurely, "Thank you. I think it's the dress."

"I meant endowed with material possessions."

She tried to giggle, which, dressed as she was, was apparently a painful undertaking, because she abruptly stopped and took another quick, shallow breath. "Eric tried his best to be a good provider."

An earthen Chinese vase now caught the doctor's eye. He bent down to examine the markings. Seemingly satisfied with his examination, the doctor straighten up. "Well, I just have two questions. First, did your husband work out?"

"Work out?"

"Do exercises. Lift weights."

"Funny you should mention it. He just received a complete set of barbells. They set us back quite a bit, but then what is money for if not to spend?" She carefully let out what Dr. Franks assumed was supposed to be a dainty laugh.

"Yes. You said a complete set. Would you say an excessive amount of weight? He was, after all, somewhat diminutive."

"Oh, Eric did nothing halfway. I mean, look at this place."

"Uh, yes. May I see them?"

"Of course." Her lips formed a smile, yet her eyes looked pained. "Could you, um, help me up the step?"

Wally met them in the hallway. More precisely, he blocked Dr. Franks, looming over and frowning down at him.

"It's all right, Wally," Mrs. Sampson said. "We'll just be a moment. He's quite protective," she added as they passed him.

Dr. Franks slowed down as they passed another painting in the hallway.

The spare bedroom was empty except for a thick pad of carpet, a weight bench and steel barbells, neatly stacked by size. The doctor looked them over.

"These are unused," he noted.

"Actually, I bought those for Eric. He had been spending so much time at the club lately." She paused to catch another breath. "I thought this might get him to stay home more."

They walked back toward the living room. Dr. Franks offered Mrs. Sampson his arm, but Wally cut between them and assisted her instead. Once back, the doctor took a seat on an ornate wooden chair by the window.

"Now regarding the, um, unfortunate accident—did the three volumes fall on him or was he by chance trying to lift them as a show of his new-found strength?"

Mrs. Sampson's mouth dropped open. "How did you know?"

"A guess."

She seemed about to say more, but then her lower lip trembled and the sides of her mouth turned down.

"Poor Eric. He was always trying to prove himself." She pulled a tissue from her purse and dabbed a dry eye. "Thankfully, I'm well provided for."

Dr. Franks stood up and coughed again. He ran his hand carefully along the arm of the chair.

"About that, madam. You may want to keep an eye on your expenses. There will be life insurance, of course, but–"

Mrs. Sampson looked up quickly.

"What are you saying? I'm loaded. Why these pearls alone–"

"Are fake. I can tell by the sound."

"Fake?" She held them up.

"As is, I'm guessing, everything in this room."

Mrs. Sampson marched over to the doctor, which was no mean feat in her dress.

"You're nuts! Look at that chair. That's a genuine Louis Quatours."

"Madam, this ain't even a Louis Prima. Also, Ming vases don't have windmills on them. The painter Paul Klee spells his name with a K not a C. And as far as I know Vermeer never did anything on black velvet."

Mrs. Sampson's eyes narrowed to dots. She balled up a fist as if about to punch him. He wondered if it was an appropriate time to ask her to a movie.

"I think you should leave," she said at last.

Dr. Franks walked to the door. Mrs. Sampson followed only as far as the step up to the foyer. Wally, who had been lurking within earshot in the hall, thrust out a dirty wad of fabric that the doctor suddenly realized was his coat.

"Just had one more question, if I may," he added as he shook out his mac. "Was your husband at all interested in ants?"

Mrs. Sampson's eyes became slits. Wally opened the door and cracked his prominent knuckles. It was time to leave.

The subway was half-filled as Dr. Franks rode back in the mid-afternoon. He settled onto a bench and began making mental notes. The late Eric Sampson had obviously been living beyond his means, or had been pretending to. The doctor had a general idea what an editor made and it wasn't enough to buy property in such a posh building, let alone furnish it. Had the man had a gambling problem? Had Mrs. Sampson been forcing them into a champagne lifestyle on a beer budget? And what about the hulking servant, Wally? Not much of a butler, and apparently more than a manservant. Something was afoot, he thought. He just had to figure out what.

The train stopped abruptly. Through the grimy window could see the Polo Grounds. Passengers came and went. The doors closed and the train lurched forward. The doctor lit a Turkish Dandy, took a long drag, and gave a thought for his now defunct 1952 Ford Crown Vic, purchased from that crook Dinky Dave and now no doubt rusting away in a Jersey City junkyard.

THE MASSIVE ORGAN

"Hey doc, did you see *Lawrence Welk* the other night? He did an accordion duet with Myron Floren. *Lady of Spain.* "

"I've told you at least a dozen times, I don't watch *Lawrence Welk*. Too much oboe."

Einstein was, as always, busily stacking publications as his white hair blew around like some hoary Medusa. Even the bricks keeping the papers from blowing away were perfectly aligned. The doctor watched patiently. He appreciated tidiness in others.

"It's supposed to get up to sixty degrees tomorrow," Einstein continued. "How 'bout that for November?"

Dr. Franks grunted. Einstein talked incessantly. Usually about the same three or four topics. He picked up the *Post* and glanced at a headline. "Wheelchair should not be hyphenated," he noted.

Einstein nodded. "I'm going on vacation in a couple weeks. Know where? Florida. How 'bout that?"

The man, by virtue of his not being a drunkard or habitual gambler like virtually every other news vendor, possessed another attribute Dr. Franks found admirable–he heard things.

"Einstein, have you ever heard of something called the Societas Homoformicidae?"

45

"No. Are they a quartet? On Lawrence Welk they had four sisters who—"

"It would be a self-improvement club."

Einstein shook his head. Hopped from one foot to the other. "No, no. Never heard of them. Are they like Toastmasters? Anyways, I'll keep my ears open. 'Course I'll be gone first week of December. I'm going on vacation to Florida. One week. Guess where? Florida. How 'bout that?"

"Thanks, Einstein."

On the subway, heading for St. Andrew's Church, Dr. Franks wondered if he should ask fewer personal questions of the next witness. On the other hand, he figured he could handle himself with any cleric in Manhattan who wasn't Irish.

He missed the Harlem stop and had to walk back to Wall Street and the church, a venerable old cathedral nestled in the shadow of the Flatiron Building. As he entered the vestibule he could tell it had seen better days. The narthex was in need of plaster, the baptistery cracked and the ambulatory begged for a good buffing. It was hard to tell about the apse, since it was taken up by the old yet majestic pipe organ.

Dr. Franks wandered up to the instrument, sat down and tentatively toed a few pedals.

"May I help you?" asked a voice.

"The Rev. William Peeples?" the doctor asked without turning.

"Yes?"

"Is this a Kegg or a Snetzler?"

"I beg your pardon?"

Dr. Franks spun around on the bench. "The organ. I'm guessing it's a Kegg, but I'd have to do some crawling around to make sure."

"I'm afraid I don't know. Mr. Harrison would know, only..." The priest hesitated. "Who are you?"

"I'm sorry. I am Dr. Franks, a consultant with the New York Police Department." He paused as his left hand searched under the lower keyboard. "You were a friend of the deceased, Lex Harrison?"

Rev. Peeples stepped up and stood near the pulpit. Tall, thin, wispy gray hair framed a rectangular face creased by deep crow's feet. Studious, the doctor surmised, or at least nearsighted.

"I knew him. A wonderful man and a great choir director. What a sad accident. You said you were with the police?"

Not totally in the present, like most pastors; pulled in many directions at once.

"This is the organ?" Dr. Franks said aloud. "It looks unmoved and in working condition.

The reverend tapped his fingers together nervously. "They set it upright just this morning. At least, we hope. It had been disconnected and tipped on its side when Mr. Harrison tried to …"

"Hope you don't mind," Dr. Franks said, nodding to the keyboard. "I played a bit in my youth. My mother was among other things a musician."

"I'm sorry, Dr....Franks, is it? Why are you here exactly? I've told everything I know to the police. One night last week I heard a loud noise and rushed over from the rectory. There was Lex, his body trapped under the organ."

"He had been trying to lift it, is that correct?"

Rev. Peeples looked away. "It's all very confusing."

The reverend seemed reluctant to answer. Whether he was hiding something or simply distracted was unclear.

Dr. Franks' hand found what it was looking for. There was a soft click. The pipes let out a wheeze that grew, transforming into the drone of a million agitated hornets.

"Try me," he said.

"Well, I—that organ hasn't been played in years."

"Just airing it out. Don't worry—I'm a professional."

This didn't mollify Peeples, but he continued anyway. "Mr. Harrison had been threatening—bragging, really—to lift that organ for the past few weeks. At first I thought he was joking, but he was so earnest about it."

"Had Mr. Harrison started working out lately? You know—exercising?"

"Yes, but no amount of exercising—I mean, that thing must weigh a ton."

"A bit more, I'd estimate." Dr. Franks pressed a low B. "So he had been working out?" The sanctuary vibrated. A hymnal slid off the pulpit.

"Yes—um, yes. He was trying to impress a young woman in the alto section."

Dr. Franks removed a card from his pocket and handed it to Rev. Peeples.

"Does that card mean anything? It was found on Mr. Harrison."

The reverend took out his reading glasses.

"Societas Homoformicidae. My Latin is a bit rusty. Society of Men Ants?"

"Antmen, yes. Have you heard of it? Did Lex ever mention it? Or insects in general?"

Dr. Franks fiddled with a button, simultaneously added G and D notes. The hornets sounded downright angry.

"Now that you mention it, he was involved in some kind of self-improvement group. I thought it was Dale Carnegie, but this name does ring a bell."

"Do you have a phone number? An address? A name?"

The reverend shook his head and handed back the card. Dr. Franks straightened up and rubbed his hands together. He had all the evidence he could ask for. Now he just needed a theory.

"Just one more question—do you mind if I play a few bars?"

The reverend balked. "I'm not really sure—"

But it was too late.

Dr. Franks attacked the keyboards with both hands. His feet mashed the pedals like a Spaniard stomping grapes. The angry buzz became a tempestuous moan. Looking like a putty-hued Phantom of the Opera, the large man flailed at the keys. The moaning became an immense, howling throb. Pedals creaked. Stops that had been frozen for years groaned in protest. Rusty pipes erupted in sound. The tonal assault threw Rev. Peeples back into the choir pew. Fearful, he covered his head with a hymnal. Dockworkers a half a mile away heard the blaring and broke for lunch. Civil Defense wardens searched for their whistles and vests. The week-minded thought Godzilla had switched continents.

Yet the doctor was only warming up.

Pipes in the higher registers now joined the acoustic melee, rasping at first like a chronic smoker chasing a bus before blasting out with a merry and ear-deafening brilliance. Mice scurried from their holes. Plaster fell like January snow. A wren's nest cannoned out of a pipe with the force of a howitzer.

And still the song continued: defiant, unrelenting, earsplitting and very, very catchy.

It was a full minute before Rev. Peeples realized the music had ended. He stood up. In the center aisle stood Dr. Franks, shuffling his feet like a shy first-grader.

"I'm a little rusty," he admitted before turning and exiting.

A teetering pew fell over. A confused bat flew smack into a stained glass window. Rev. Peeples didn't notice. After a long moment, the cleaning lady rushed in from a side entrance. She surveyed the scene then threw a questioning glance at the reverend.

"That was the greatest performance of Jingle Bells I've ever heard," he said.

THE CASE SOLVED

"What in the heck in Hades are you trying to pull, Franks?"

Inspector Grimes, not a morning person on the sunniest of days, seemed extra surly this Friday.

"I've been taking calls since yesterday afternoon about your hijinx. Breaking furniture uptown, creating civil unrest downtown. Jimmy Fulch has the mayor breathing down my collar about you."

Dr. Franks, sitting opposite the angry inspector, refrained from expressing his surprise. Grimes was obviously beyond reason. He offered the inspector half of his Popsicle but it did nothing to soothe the man. Instead, Inspector Grimes was eyeing him with malice and what could only be described as suspicion.

"Does he want his club sandwich back?"

The muscles in the inspector's face stretched tight as bowstrings. A wiggly white worm of skin writhed atop the beet red of his forehead. It seemed to the doctor that a few specs of blood had appeared in the whites of the man's eyes. "Club sandwich!? Are you trying to get me fired? I mean, is that your plan? Did they send you from downtown to force me out?

"In my defense, I think I made solid progress on the case. And that church ceiling was due for a new paint job no matter what."

Inspector Grimes bit clear through his cigar stub, an inch of which dropped into his coffee and bobbed like a gangrenous finger. He let out something between a choke and a sob as he tried to fish it out, and then, giving up, jabbed a wet digit at the doctor.

"You! You have until five o'clock today to give me some evidence that any of these accidents are murders or you're off the case!"

Dr. Franks, sensing the meeting was at an end, stood up, wrapped the Popsicle in his hanky and stuffed it into his left pocket.

"Any way we can push that back to Monday? Today is laundry day and—"

"Get out!"

The doctor got halfway to the exit before circling back. Inspector Grimes was again trying to fish out the chunk of cigar.

"Um, I was wondering if I could get an advance. I'm short on cash and need a new graduated cylinder."

He ducked the coffee mug just in time.

At 10 a.m. he stopped at Ace-Descent Laboratory Supply and put a graduated cylinder on layaway. It was a nice one with an adjustable blue ring. An oversized magnifying glass in the display window caught his attention, not because of its size so much as its focusing the sunlight into a beam that was burning through a lab coat. He pointed this out to the proprietor, hoping the man would give him a generous discount. No dice.

Passing through Greenwich Village, he soon arrived at Wang's Cajun Deli—only to find it closed. He checked his wristwatch and realized it had stopped working at 12:02 a.m.

the previous night (4:02 a.m. GMT). The billboard at Times Square, however, indicated it was a quarter past eleven.

A thin old man with a large head and exaggerated features was carefully sweeping the sidewalk in front of the door, making small, quick attacks at the cement as if intent on brushing away microscopic enemies. Dr. Franks realized it was the cook, Uncle Tonoose.

"What's happened?" the doctor stuttered when he drew within a few feet of the man. "Is George sick?"

Uncle Tonoose raised his head slowly. "He sold it."

A hundred and one questions raced through the doctor's brain at once. All that came out was "Sold it?"

"Yeah. Sold it. I guess someone finally offered him a hundred dollars American for the place. He's moving back to Greece."

"Greece? I thought he was Lebanese."

The old man resumed his sweeping. "Yeah. He never liked that about you."

There was nothing for it but to head home. Not having secured an advance he didn't even bother trying to flag down a taxi.

The sun and the unseasonably warm weather did little to brighten his mood. He needed to solve the case. Today. That was the only way he was going to establish the field of homoscience, get a hefty retainer from the police department for future consulting work and, most importantly, finally be able to move out of his mother's house and into a place where he and his molecule could live unmolested.

Mrs. Franks was less than thrilled when he hinted that he might be off the case.

"Ever since your dear father passed away seventeen years ago I've only wanted two things," she yelled from the kitchen where she was ironing washcloths. "That you be happy and that I be able to convert your bedroom into a parlor where I can take visitors."

Taking visitors. Dr. Franks shook his head. The only visitors she ever took were the members of her bridge club, and the only thing she took was their laundry money.

The can opener profits were still nowhere to be found. Cousin Phelps had explained over the phone, rather cryptically the doctor felt, that the funds were tied up due to "interstate commerce regulations."

Down in the basement, he checked his rack of test tubes. Each of the four contained a pale green fluid—solutions he had created from the residue on the separate pieces of evidence: pica stick, pencil, baton and business cards. The fact that the fluids were similar in color was a good sign. A half hour later he had the results. As he had suspected, each tube bore traces of formic acid, cinnamon and a strong hallucinogen. Solid evidence, but of what?

He picked up his slide whistle.

Too many clues, he thought, tootling. And yet not enough. Were these murders? If so, to what end? In the case of Jimmy and Jacky Fulch perhaps jealousy over a stolen woman, or simply sibling rivalry. And Mrs. Sampson could have been playing dumb about her finances. If so, she was certainly convincing. Perhaps she did it for the insurance. And there were always reasons for killing an accountant. The doctor had not infrequently considered murdering Cousin Phelps. But the choir director?

He drew out the arm of the whistle, producing a long, descending note.

The problem was that everyone had a reason to kill somebody but nobody had a reason to kill everybody. And the one thing tying them together—ants—indicated nothing.

Dash's bowl of cereal, Dr. Franks noted, remained exactly where he had left it that morning: on the top shelf by the basement window, unmoved and untouched. Outside in the yard the husky squirrel leaned awkwardly against the elm tree. Perhaps what the critter needed was a good Swanson TV Dinner, complete with apple compote.

The doctor trilled an improvisational arpeggio.

"Bernie!" his mother called down. "Stop playing that damn thing! Geez, it goes right through you!"

Dr. Franks frowned. He was out of time. There was only one thing to do. It was a long-shot, but...

He picked up the basement phone and dialed. "Grimes. Dr. Franks. Wait—don't hang up. Listen, I've solved the case. That's right. Just bring all the principals to my place tonight at 9 p.m. No, I'm not kidding." He listened and then sighed. "Yes, I know if I'm screwing with you it will be my butt in the sling. Great! 9 p.m. And can your boys verify a few things for me...?"

Officer Marvin Dingle stood, vaguely rigid and alert, in front of the small but well-maintained home of Mrs. Margaret Franks. Were one able to see through the hard cast and skin of the man's left hand they would notice hairline fractures to the lunate, triquetrum and pisiform, as well as a clean break in the fifth metacarpal bone. Dingle absentmindedly scratched his forehead with his right hand and immediately winced in pain. The lump on his cranium had gone down, but the tenderness remained. What's more, the wincing made his ribs ache, tightly wrapped though they were, and also sent a sharp pain along the stitched laceration traversing his lower back. The worst pain of all, though, came from the memory of his wife's reaction upon hearing about the accident. *You got hit by a taxi, again, while bending down to pick up a quarter—and you didn't even get the quarter? That is just like you, Dingle.* The sergeant looked up into the clear night sky. A broken streetlight afforded him a clearer view of the stars than was usual. So many stars. So vast a universe. Why, he wondered, was it picking on him, of all people? And why, for that matter, did he think the universe owed him anything? It seemed that the only time he actually thought about such things was when something bad happened to him (though in his case that was fairly often). Which reminded him of the old saw that there were no atheists in foxholes. Perhaps, he thought, it wasn't that people turned to God for help in such times but needed someone to blame. Who, after all, stopped to thank God when things were going well? He strolled a few steps toward the next row house, where a metal railing protected a basement stairwell. Sergeant Dingle looked up again, trying to remember the last time things had gone well for him. Perhaps it was that cold day last winter when his wife had made him that warm, sweet-smelling hot cocoa—right before it scalded his tongue. Or their honeymoon in Miami—at least that first day, before Hurricane Hazel made landfall. As he looked up, pondering those brief moments of happiness, a fateful glop of pigeon poop hit him in the eye, causing him to stumble over the railing and fall down to the Kleisterman's front door.

Inside, Dr. Franks was making final preparations for the conference, which consisted solely of spraying Lysol in an attempt to mask the last evidence of the salmon cakes his mother had burned for dinner. Mrs. Franks herself was out attending a Daughters of Erin dinner; she wasn't Irish, but did enjoy soda bread and Irish coffee.

THE CASE DISSOLVED

The first guest, Rev. Peeples, knocked meekly at 8:55. By 9:15, all the principals had arrived and were playing a sort of musical chairs in the cramped basement. Mrs. Sampson, the editor's widow, and Miss Chanelle, witness from the Mishnick mimeograph mishap, sat on a wooden chair and the faulty electric chair (now covered with a yellow wool blanket), respectively. Jimmy Fulch had commandeered Dr. Franks' office chair, having given up the electric chair to the Miss Chanelle. Behind them, in reverse order and uncomfortably sharing a wobbly plywood bench, were Inspector Grimes, Rev. Peeples and Mrs. Sampson's morose servant, Wally. Einstein, who had served the coffee, sat off to the side on the old air conditioner. The news vendor had been only too happy to help. "Maybe I can type up this case too," he told the doctor. "I'm up to thirty words a minute. Did you read the other one I gave you?"

Dr. Franks, chairless, paced uncertainly between the staircase and his worktable.

"Just a quick announcement before we begin," he said. "If you're drinking from the good china please do be careful. If it's the stuff with kittens on it, not so much."

"Inspector Grimes, can we get this over with?" It was Mrs. Sampson, who was dressed provocatively enough to give Miss Chanelle a run for her money. "If I'd have known I was going to see this oaf again," she indicated Dr. Franks, "I wouldn't have come."

The others grumbled their agreement. Jimmy Fulch leaned back on the office chair. A spring popped.

"I got a question. What are these things? They're pretty tasty." He was snacking out of a yellow melamine bowl.

"Those are, um–"

"Holy crud! There's a beaver at the window," Miss Chanelle cried.

Outside the cellar window above Dr. Franks' work table a large gray rodent was attempting to claw its way in.

"Please. That's only Dash, my pet squirrel. He's a little upset because Mr. Fulch is eating from his bowl."

Mr. Fulch did a professionally comedic spit-take. A damp piece of Trix flew across the room and landed on Einstein's shoe.

"Mercy–are you sure it's not a woodchuck?" Rev. Peeples asked.

"And am I crazy or is it clutching its chest?" Grimes asked, eyeing the creature with suspicion.

Dr. Franks held up his hands. "If we could please get back to the matter at hand." When they had settled down, he continued. "I appreciate your time and your patience. I even appreciate your anger with me. This has been a very difficult time for all of you, and as Inspector Grimes will agree this has been a very complicated case."

"You're on own on this one, doc," Grimes said as he fought for more room on the bench.

"But I am happy to say that I have solved it using the newly-founded discipline of homoscience." He paused and, for once, there was no tittering. "Ladies and gentlemen, by the end of this evening I will reveal the identity of the murderer."

This was met with a louder chorus of grumbling. It was the first any of them had heard about murder.

"Perhaps I should make introductions all around. Rev. William Peeples, friend and co-worker of the late choir director, Lex Harrison, whose death was, as they say, a clerical error."

He paused. No one laughed.

"Mrs. Linda Sampson, widow of Eric, who met his untimely demise under the *Oxford English Dictionary*, and her servant, whose name I can't recall."

"Wally," Mrs. Sampson said.

"So you admit you know his name!"

"Of course. He's my servant."

"Interesting. Next, the lovely Miss Chanelle, co-worker of the unfortunate accountant, Mr. Mishnick, whose life ended mimeographically." Again, no laughter. "The famous Jimmy Fulch, whose diminutive brother has left this earthly stage for an eternal one. Inspector Grimes you are all familiar with."

"Hi!" Einstein said. "They call me Einstein. I like *The Lawrence Welk Show*. Guess where I'm going for vacation."

"Shut up, Einstein."

Outside the window, Dash coughed and spit out a tooth.

"Four deaths: by organ, by encyclopedia, by office machine and by um, Mr. Fulch."

"Yeah, and all accidents," Fulch said. "What's this about murder?"

"In due time," Dr. Franks said, holding out a palm to quiet him.

A siren sounded. Inspector Grimes went to the window facing the street and peered out.

"Dingle?" Franks said.

Grimes nodded. "Carry on." He resumed his seat.

"One of the detective's fine officers is bringing the final piece of the puzzle. In the meantime—the commonalities." Dr. Franks unveiled a chalkboard containing several names, as well as a small column of words: *pound cake, Bosco, Brylcreem, boxer shorts (XL), Klondike Bars.* "Ignore this part–it's for my mother. Now. You'll notice that in all four cases, the victims were small men. In all cases they were crushed by heavy objects–objects they were purported to have tried to lift in a show of manly vigor. In all cases, the men had on their person this card: Societas Homoformicidae. Society of the Antmen."

"I'm bored. Can I leave?" Miss Chanelle asked, checking her watch.

"We have as yet been unable to identify this organization; however, we do know it is a self-improvement program targeting small, weak men."

"I don't understand all this," Mrs. Sampson said. Her lower lip began to quiver. "Are you saying this group killed my dear Eric?" She inhaled sharply as if she were about to cry. Rev. Peeples offered his hanky, but Mrs. Sampson's servant blocked him and offered his own cloth, which could only be called a snot rag.

"Not at all, my dear. Not at all. Lex Harrison's death, I believe, was a sad accident, induced by overconfidence from his participation in this secret society. We know, for instance, that all the victims had begun working out. Lifting weights. I believe that, buoyed by overconfidence and hallucinogenic stimulants provided by this self-improvement club, Mr. Harrison tried to lift the church organ, only to have it crush him when his strength failed."

The reverend shook his head. "How horrible."

Dr. Franks thought for a moment, and then added *Cremora* to the shopping list.

"Which brings us to the curious case of Eric Sampson, senior editor at Encyclopedia Britannica." He wheeled on the widow. "Mrs. Sampson, is it not true that your husband was spending well beyond his means?"

Mrs. Sampson stared back, stone-faced.

"Is it not true that he owed several bookies, and had sold off your expensive furnishings and jewelry to pay for his gambling debts? Don't deny it—we have proof."

"Yes!" she cried, breaking down for real this time. "He was broke. We were broke."

Wally stood and glared menacingly at the doctor.

"Is it not also true that you are close to your mysterious servant here? Obviously, he's not much of a servant."

"That's a horrible thing to say."

"Your relationship is more than professional, is it not?"

Mrs. Sampson jumped up. "What are you implying?"

"I imply nothing. I state that you and he hatched a plan to get rid of your husband and collect the insurance. You read about Mr. Harrison's death and somehow learned that he was a member of this Society of Antmen. You knew your husband was also a member. And you rigged it to make it look like a similar accidental death."

Jimmy Fulch jumped up.

"Now I know this guy's a loon," he said to Inspector Grimes. "This is worse than the plot to our famous movie *Balloons over Bologna.*"

"Sit down, Mr. Fulch," the doctor demanded. "You're next."

Mr. Fulch dropped his large frame back into the office chair, which gave a sad groan and listed to one side.

"You too had a problem. Jimmy and Jacky were on the skids. What's more, you were tied into a twenty-year deal at the Comedy Cavalcade. It was a good deal in 1940, but a mere pittance in today's economy. Further, you had an offer to host a new game show called *Who Wants a Dollar?* You and only you. So you had to get rid of the contract and your brother Jacky. And his death would cancel both obligations."

Fulch jumped back up. "What the hell—!"

"You read about the choir director's death. Then you heard about the editor's death. Both apparent accidents, and both victims members of the same oddball society."

They waited as the siren blared again, then faded as Dingle's ambulance drove away.

"But what about this Mishnick fellow?" the reverend asked.

"Fulch was a smart guy. He knew that, being a celebrity, there would probably be a thorough investigation. That is, unless his brother's death was part of murder spree–a Midget Murder Spree. So he arranged the Mishnick death."

"How?" Mrs. Sampson asked.

Inspector Grimes scratched his head. "Yeah, how?" He seemed interested despite himself.

"Through his old friend, Miss Chanelle."

"I've never met this woman in my life," Fulch objected.

"What are we doing now?" asked Miss Chanelle, who had been inspecting her nose in a compact.

"Don't deny it," Dr. Franks said. "We have photos of your tryst last month, taken by a private eye hired by one of your ex-wives."

He handed a photo each to Fulch and Chanelle. Fulch's face lit up.

"Oh yeah, baby! I remember you. In the back room at the Four Seasons."

A look of recognition came to Miss Chanelle's face. "Gosh, my hair was longer then." She looked at Fulch. "Hey, Jerry honey!"

"It's Jimmy."

"No. It's Jerry. I'm good with names. Numbers, not so much."

Dr. Franks felt that he was losing the room.

"Sooo, having established that connection, I will continue. It was a simple matter for Miss Chanelle to sneak you into the Excelsior Bowling Apparel Co. Ltd. office, lure Mr. Mishnick into the supply room and help you drop the mimeograph machine on him."

The cacophonous doorbell sounded. Einstein went upstairs to answer it.

"Then, having established this pattern of, shall we say, accidental suicides, you had but to wait a few days before jumping on top of your brother."

The servant stood up and blew something out of his nose. He then cleared his throat and said, "Truly, that is the most farfetched theory ever proposed."

"It speaks!" Dr. Franks said, taken aback.

A police officer came down the stairs, crossed to Inspector Grimes, handed him a folded piece of paper and whispered something in his ear.

"Here is the piece of evidence that ties it all together," the doctor said, gesturing to the policemen. "I assume it confirms that Jimmy Fulch ran out prior to the first show on the night of Mr. Mishnick's death, arriving back some half hour later."

Inspector Grimes coughed. "No. It says he was having dinner at the time of the death."

Dr. Franks laughed nervously. "Ha. Alone, no doubt, with no one to verify his alibi."

"He was dining with Leonard Bernstein and Sammy Cahn. Oh—and the mayor."

Dr. Franks went a little pale. "Well, Leonard Bernstein. He's a little iffy. Have you heard the philharmonic's version of Mahler's Fifth? Weak on the percussion."

Inspector Grimes coughed loudly. "Not only that, doc, but that whole antmen thing was never in the papers. So that's another hole in your theory."

"Okay, I apologize to Mr. Fulch. But I'm still right about Mrs. Sampson and her servant. He's not really your servant, is he?"

"No," Mrs. Sampson said. She rushed over and gave the servant a hug. "He's my brother. He's helping out while working on his doctoral thesis at NYU."

"Yes, um, helping out by killing your husband for the insurance."

"Doctor, we come from a rich family."

Dr. Franks was starting to feel light-headed.

"But—but you told me you didn't come from old money."

"I don't. But my father invented the electric can opener. He's been swimming in royalties for the past year."

Dr. Franks gaped. "Wait! I invented the electric can opener."

"Oh! You're the guy that suggested they put the knife sharpener on the back and sell it in designer colors."

Dr. Franks looked down. His shoulders sagged.

"I haven't seen a dime yet."

The group marched up the stairs in twos. Mr. Fulch invited Miss Chanelle and the rest to Sardi's for a nightcap. Einstein patted Dr. Franks on the shoulder. Inspector Grimes stopped just long enough to say, "You're off the case."

Upstairs there was a commotion. A woman's voice shouted.

"What the hell—is that my good china!?"

DR. FRANKS AND
THE WELL-ENDOWED DOWAGER

Years earlier, when Dr. Franks was not a doctor but only Bernie Franks, promising and well-groomed undergraduate student at one of colleges at Oxford or perhaps Cambridge, there lived a wealthy English dowager who wanted to travel to South Africa. Being a wealthy dowager, she could make that happen. The Dowager Emerald Pense, Lady of Voir Dire Abbey, Worcestershire Adjacent, had booked several adjoining staterooms aboard the *RMS Neuralgia,* a twin-screw passenger ship headed for Cape Town by way of St. Helena. Now well into her forties (no one dared ask how well), Dowager Dire Abbey was anything but demure. An American by birth, she had met the late Earl when he attended one of her theatrical performances at a way-off-Broadway venue. Emerald Starr, as she was billed in those days, was known for her emotive acting style and curvaceous figure, and was not uncommonly referred to as the Sarah Bernhardt of Burlesque by hawkers on the Lower East Side. The earl, a high-born man with rather low-brow tastes, was smitten after her first (some would say overly deep) bow concluding her starring turn in a production cleverly titled *Cleopatra's Asp.* Two months later, to the horror of nearly everyone, they were married in the family chapel at Voir Dire

Abbey. Despite familial opposition, the couple enjoyed a decade and a half of marital bliss. They were, after all, young, rich, healthy and by all accounts deeply in love. Between their nuptials in 1917 and the earl's untimely death in 1935 (in a freak croquet accident) they were only apart for six months, when the Earl of Voir Dire Abbey answered the call of duty and served as aide de camp to Gen. Haig during the first battle of Ypres, dutifully picking out proper attire for both day and night campaigns against the Bosch.

The trip to South Africa, officially to inspect an estate the Dowager had recently inherited on her husband's side of the family, was also seen as a chance for her to once and for all put the unpleasantness of the earl's demise behind her. Among her traveling companions were the dowager's personal servant, Julia, her late husband's brother-in-law, the Count du Compte, and a surly bull mastiff named Lady Ashton who does not figure into this tale. Some among the retinue were less thrilled about the adventure than others, as became evident the third night at sea.

"What's wrong—don't like the fish?" the Dowager asked. She had just delivered a rather bawdy punch line to a story involving Mae West and a plumber and had noticed the Count was the only one not laughing. Rather, he was scowling at his plate and poking carefully at the contents as if it were evidence at a crime scene. He had a face that scowled easily: narrow features and deep creases around the nose and mouth. His entire frame, in fact, was unnaturally slender, as if someone had pressed him in a book like a flower.

"I hope the Captain will take no offense," he announced with more pleasure than regret, "but I have had better grilled sand dabs meuniere."

The Dowager let loose with a harsh, masculine *ha* that attracted the attention of half the diners in the banquet room. "As my mom used to say, If you don't like it you can starve. I myself had two helpings and would have had a third if not for this durn corset. It's squeezing me tighter than a python on its honeymoon!"

The others at the captain's table smiled weakly and/or exchanged embarrassed glances.

"Honestly!" the Count said. "That is no language for the table. Or, for that matter, a lady."

The Dowager threw up her jewel-bedecked hands as if hurt and said, "Who's a lady?" Then she let loose with another booming laugh.

"Count du Compte," the Captain said, "perhaps the storm is upsetting your constitution. Would another dish be to your liking?"

"Ah, don't pay him no mind, Captain. It's not how it tastes that bothers him. It's how much it costs."

"Madam!"

"Now don't get all offended, County." She turned to the others. "He's a good egg, really. It's just that as executor of my late husband's estate he worries about me losing all my money. It's silly, really. Do I look like I'm going broke?"

It was true that everything about her said money, from the large pearl earrings hanging from her delicate ear lobes to the ostrich feather boa wrapped about her smooth porcelain neck to the richly brocaded evening dress to the three ruby rings on her right hand and the large diamond wedding band on her left. The dowager, despite her age, was still stunningly beautiful, and if she had gained a few pounds it only added to her allure, hinting at an appetite for sensual pleasures.

Mr. Jenks, a rather uncouth gentlemen sitting directly opposite the Dowager, was the first to respond.

"That's quite a chunk of glass you've got around your neck, if I may be so bold to say, your Ladyship." He pointed at her with his salad fork, which he was using to eradicate his Bismarck herring.

The others at the captain's table knew immediately to what Mr. Jenks was referring: a deep red ruby hanging from a silver chain. It was rectangular in shape, the size of a child's fist, resting on the Dowager's breastbone.

"Oh this little thing. They call it the Eye of Dire Abbey. Quite valuable, I'm told."

Mr. Jenks smiled. "A replica, to be sure. The real one must be somewhere safe."

"If so, it is a near-perfect copy," said a young man with a harsh American accent. This diner, handsome and clean-shaven, with short blond hair brushed carefully back, leaned forward to get a better look. The Dowager accommodated him by leaning forward herself, presenting not just the jewel but her ample décolletage.

"Do you like what you see, Mr. Franks?"

For that is who the young man was. Mr. Bernard Franks: undergraduate, co-captain of the archery team and solo cruise ship passenger. His father, Major Wendell Franks (Ret.) was an old friend of the Captain, which is how the younger Franks found himself at the head table.

Franks blushed at the Dowager's double-entendre. Then his eyes widened. "Good Lord!"

"You know your baubles, young man. You are correct—it is the real McCoy. I'll have no truck with paste. Had enough of the fake stuff in my theater days. Mind you, it's hard to tell the difference."

"Just the same, you needn't flaunt it about," the Count said, jabbing disdainfully at his pickled beets. "Unlike your other assets."

The Dowager had once quipped that she did not feel dressed in anything but a low-cut dress, a statement her onboard wardrobe readily confirmed.

"I must agree with the Count," the Captain said. "In any event we will do everything in our power to ensure the Lady's trip is a safe and secure one."

After dinner Franks took a walk around the deck. The wind was howling and the sea was choppy—as it had been since they left England. The moon was nearly full and, when it broke through the quickly moving clouds, bathed the ship in a soft glow.

"Storm approaching from the southwest," the Bursar told Franks as he headed for his stateroom. "A big one, if I'm not mistaken."

Franks changed into his white tie and tails for the evening and headed back to the main salon. Rough seas did not worry him. His father, Major Wendell Franks (Ret.), was a noted explorer and his mother a famed aviatrix. Storms, floods, earthquakes and wild animals were as common to the young Franks as model trains and hobby horses to most children. He could not in fact remember experiencing calm seas.

There were few passengers in the salon. Most of the others, the Captain explained, had decided to ride out the approaching storm in their cabins. But the Dowager was there, along with the always dour Count. She was sitting on an upholstered chair that had been pulled up to a game table.

"Mr. Franks, join us for cards! You play canasta, I assume. We'll be partners."

He seated himself across from the Dowager.

"Will there be a fourth?"

"Hope so. Count, see if you can scrounge somebody up."

The count rose uncertainly and headed for the door.

"And tell Julia to come out here," she called after him. "Whatcha drinking?" This last to Franks.

"Sherry. Just a touch."

"I'm a scotch man myself," the Dowager said. She took a hearty sip from her tumbler to prove her point.

"Count du Compte seems rather unhappy."

"He's in mourning. Sadly, his wife, the Lady Henry, died at the same time as my dear Henry, the Earl. They were brother and sister, you see."

"And they died in a croquet accident."

"Tragic, yet all too common the Count says. I would have died too if I hadn't at that moment ducked into the conservatory for a quick nip. The Earl didn't approve of mixing alcohol and athletics. Ah, Julia!"

A pretty black woman, about the same age as the Dowager, appeared at the table. She was dressed as a servant, but her body language, fists shoved into her hips and head to one side, was decidedly unservantlike.

"What you want now, your highness? Your pillow need fluffing or something?"

The Dowager removed all her rings save her wedding band and handed them to the other woman.

"Put these somewhere safe, will you? It's hard to deal cards with all these rocks on my fingers."

"I'd think it would be hard to use a fork too, but that weren't any problem." Julia stuffed the rings in her apron pocket. Her hands went back on her hips, and her head tilted to the other side. "Will that be all, your Ladyship? I was just settling down with a good book and a warm blanket when your Count rousted me."

"No. Go back to your book, Julia. I'll stop by later and explain all the big words to you."

"Oh, ha ha, your Ladyship. You are in top form tonight!"

Julia stomped away.

"You have an interesting relationship with your maid," Franks ventured after a long silence.

"Oh, me and Julia go way back. My best friend. She was with me in New York." She leaned forward provocatively. "I did mention my days treading the boards?"

Franks reddened. "Er."

"Between you and me I miss the old life. This upper class nonsense ain't as fun as it looks. You ever live in a country estate? Dusty old things. Cold as a witch's bum in the winter too. And the Count always on my case about money. Like it was his." She thought for a moment. "I guess it could have been if things had gone different. Aw, but enough about old me. What takes you to South Africa?"

"Family, I guess you'd say. I'm meeting up with my father for an expedition."

"That's right—you're Wendell Franks' boy, ain't you? And Patty Price's too? She broke a few of Amelia Earhart's records, didn't she?"

"Yes. Mother broke a few of Lindbergh's as well."

"And his heart, from what I hear." She leaned back and sighed. "Gave it all up for wedded bliss, eh? Well, I know the feeling. It's a hard choice, I'll tell you. Ah, Count—found a fourth I see."

The Count approached with Mr. Jenks.

"I'm the best he could do, I'm afraid, your Ladyship. Looks like most people are battening down for the storm."

"You'll do." The Dowager looked him up and down. "You'll do fine."

The game progressed in a friendly fashion, at least among the three who were not the Count. The rising storm was not helping the latter's mood.

"Your Ladyship knows it is against the rules to look through the discards." he chided coldly.

"Just straightening the pile, County. Your turn, Bernie. So what line are you in, Mr. Jenks?"

"Oh. I'm in the moving business, you might say. Moving things here and there."

Bernie Franks raised a well-trimmed eyebrow. "You must be of some importance to be placed at the Captain's table."

"Oh no, not me, sir. Just friends with the Captain. Business acquaintances, you might say."

"Speaking of acquaintances—who was that young girl I saw you talking to earlier, Bernie?"

Franks, who had been organizing his hand, stared blankly at the Dowager.

"Oh! The young lady. Miss Gertrude von Kapukt, I believe."

"A university student at Heidelberg University," Mr. Jenks said.

"She's got quite a honker. No offense."

Mr. Jenks laid down several melds, using four wild 3s. His partner, the Count, offered a rare smile.

"So you ended up with all the 3s, and the bonus," the Dowager said. "What luck."

"Perhaps tonight is my lucky night."

Franks took his turn and tried to catch the Dowager's eye so she would see what meld he was putting down, but she was exchanging glances with Mr. Jenks. The Count took a card and immediately put his hand down.

"I'm out."

Jenks rose and stretched. "Well played, Count. We make a good team. May I get you another scotch, your Ladyship?"

"No, no. Four's my limit. I'll sleep like a log tonight."

Franks hesitated. He wasn't sure if he should broach the subject. "That being the case, perhaps you should put the Eye of Dire Abbey in the Captain's safe."

"Ha!" She polished off the last two fingers of her drink. "I'd like to see someone try to take it off me." She rose with surprising steadiness, considering the storm and the potables. "Gentlemen, it has been swell."

The Dowager and Mr. Jenks headed off for their rooms. Franks lagged behind with the Count.

"I shouldn't have said anything," Franks said. "It's not my business."

"No. I've warned her many times myself. I've warned her of the consequences if the Eye is lost, but—well, you see how she is."

The Count never took his eyes off the Dowager as he spoke, but whether his expression was one of concern or contempt, Franks could not determine.

THE EYE OF VOIR DIRE ABBEY

Waves crashed. Wind howled. The ship pitched erratically. Bernie Franks was asleep as soon as his handsome head hit his downy pillow. The intensity of the storm and the resulting commotion had no effect on his rest. Shouts of alarm and barked orders from the crew on deck and moans of passengers rushing out to divest themselves of the evening meal were incorporated into his dreams as cries of delight from fellow riders in a wild fox hunt.

Much later, he awoke with a feeling something was not right. It was quiet; the storm had abated. Suddenly, the door to his cabin flew open and a figure entered, silhouetted by the hallway lights. The person staggered a bit, but remained at the threshold.

Franks uttered the first words that came to mind. "May I help you?"

"Bloody hell—wrong room!" a man's voice cursed. And without another word, the visitor left.

Franks started to pull himself up to lock the door, then fell back, dizzy. Odd, he thought, I don't remember drinking more than a touch of sherry. As he tossed fitfully, he identified the visitor's voice as that of Mr. Jenks.

The next morning brought horrible news: breakfast would be delayed twenty minutes due to the storm. Also, the Eye of Dire Abbey was missing.

Franks came upon the Dowager and her retinue in the salon where they had played cards the previous night. The Captain was conferring with the trio of the Dowager, Count du Compte and the servant, Julia. Though well-scrubbed and wearing a clean, starched uniform, the man had bloodshot eyes and puffy bags underneath them. Indeed, between the storms and the missing jewel the Captain had had little rest.

"It's gone, I tell you," the Dowager was saying, apparently in response to a question by the Captain. "Julia and I have searched everywhere, right Julia?"

Julia, dressed in the same maid's outfit as the night before, was shaking her head dramatically. "That's right. Ladyship and me have been turning her stateroom upside down all morning. All we found was the silver chain it used to be attached to."

"The last thing I want to say is I told you so, but...," the Count said with obvious satisfaction.

Bernie sat down at the first open chair, a few yards from the others. His legs felt wobbly and his stomach uneven despite having emptied itself in the pre-dawn hours (and ruining his robe and nightshirt). He had cut himself so many times while shaving his face was now a blizzard of toilet paper.

"I don't understand it," the Dowager continued. "It didn't leave my neck all night. I was even wearing it when–" She paused abruptly. "And when I woke up this morning it was gone!"

She raised a hand to her breast where the jewel had rested the night before. Franks noticed, despite his queasiness (*what had he eaten last night?*), the Dowager was now dressed more conservatively, in a dark blue dress with a white lace collar buttoned to the top.

"Now your Ladyship. Don't you worry," Julia said, patting her on the shoulder. "I'm sure we'll find that old rock."

"And I'm sure the Captain is doing everything in his power to find it," the Count added.

The Dowager looked up to the ceiling, imploringly. "Oh Lord, what will I do? First I lost Henry and now the Eye of Dire Abbey. Can any other evil befall this family?" She hugged herself and began moaning.

Julia instantly offered her a handkerchief and more words of consolation. The Count rose and gestured for the Captain and Bernie Franks to join him. Reluctantly, Franks rose to his feet and stumbled after.

"I cannot impress upon you, er—what happened to your face?"

"Shaving accident," Franks mumbled.

"No, I mean it's green and blotchy."

"He'll be fine," the Captain said, slapping him robustly between the shoulder blades. "Pray continue."

Franks' stomach lurched. Two blood-stained bits of toilet paper fell to the floor.

"Well—" The Count watched Bernie's googlily eyes cross and uncross before continuing. "I was stressing the importance of finding this jewel."

"I assure you, Count, that I am doing everything possible."

The Count coughed and added in a hushed voice, "The matter goes beyond the loss of the ruby, which is priceless. Um—" He glanced at Franks. "Perhaps you would excuse us?"

"Certainly!" Bernie told his white oxfords (looking up was making him dizzy or, rather, dizzier). He braced himself on the back of a loveseat and took a step away.

The Captain grabbed him by the elbow. "If it pertains to the matter at hand I would prefer Bernie hear it. I have been in many a scrape with Major Franks and trust both him and his son implicitly."

"Really. I don't mind," Bernie said, possibly not aloud.

"The Eye of Dire Abbey, as you may know, was given to the family by King George III."

"Is anybody else losing consciousness?" Franks heard himself ask.

The Captain nodded for the Count to continue.

"More precisely, the jewel was put in the family's care as a token of the Crown's trust. If it is lost—and this is the key point—the family loses all titles and privileges, including the estate of Voir Dire Abbey itself.

"So you see, it is essential you find the jewel."

"Cuban?" The Captain opened a box and held it toward Bernie Franks. The two had retired to the Captain's quarters where the officer had made quick work of a breakfast of poached eggs, smoked salmon, toast and marmalade.

"No, I'm happy just cradling this trash can."

"Ironic that you'd be sick the minute we run into clear weather. Perhaps you need some hair of the dog that bit you."

After a few minutes of contemplative puffing the Captain continued. "I hope you don't mind me roping you into all this, Bernie, but I understand from your father that we share a common interest."

"I noticed."

Even bent double as he was, Franks could see the bookshelf that filled the bulkhead to the right of the Captain. In addition to the expected items—volumes on maritime law, navigational charts, books of military history and souvenirs from exotic ports of call—there were a surprising number of crime novels. On the floor beside it, there being no other place for them, sat a stack of well-thumbed issues of *The Strand*.

"Do you not, in addition to your rigorous studies in philosophy, physics and chemistry, dabble in crime detection?"

Franks gave the bookcase a more careful examination. Volumes by Poe, Christie, Chesterton and Hodgson predominated.

"But really—I'm not a detective. At most I've tracked down a few lost cats or identified a larcenous gardener. I've never worked on a real crime."

"Ah! But neither have I," the Captain said, rising suddenly. "Father Brown, Poirot, Dupin—I've read them all. So, no doubt, have you. This is our chance to put what we've learned to the test."

Closing his eyes made him feel slightly better, Franks discovered. He took a few shallow breaths, which also helped. A real case. It was tempting. But in his present condition so was suicide.

"Captain," he said deliberately. "I appreciate your confidence in me. But I am a rank amateur."

"The first thing we have to do is identify the victims. I mean, the suspects." The Captain was lost in his musings and simultaneously leafing through an illustrated copy of *Murders in the Rue Morgue*. "Or perhaps we should concentrate first on motive. That would narrow down the list of suspects. Now who would have reason to steal a priceless ruby?"

Bernie Franks stood up, brushing invisible ashes off his immaculate waistcoat. "I think it best I leave this to you."

The Captain was now leafing through Chesterton's *The Paradoxes of Mr. Pond.* "The psychology of the principals is important too. Some peculiarity of human nature might be the key to solving this puzzle."

Franks stopped at the hatchway. "After all, you seem eminently qualified for the task."

"What did Sherlock Holmes always used to say? First, eliminate the dog that didn't bark...?"

Franks pulled himself up. "I'm sure you'll be fine."

"...and you'll have the hound of the Baskervilles. Something like that."

Franks sighed heavily. "I'll help you on one condition."

"Name it."

"Let me go on deck and throw up!"

CRIME WAVE ON
THE RMS NEURALGIA

The facts were these. There were only five people who had had access to the corridor leading to the Dowager's suite of cabins (seven if you included the Captain and Bernie Franks): the Count du Compte, Mr. Jenks, Gertrude von Kapukt, the Dowager and her servant Julia. The Dowager's quarters could be entered by a single hatchway at the end of the passageway. Julia's small cabin, which adjoined the Dowager's, had a separate entrance. Next to that was Franks' cabin. Opposite those were the Count's (next to but not adjoining the Dowager's), Mr. Jenks' and Gertrude's. The cabin boy–a trustworthy seaman who had been stationed during the night at the only access to the passageway–insisted he had seen no one enter or leave, although he had heard a man's voice just before seven bells, or 3:30 am. Since the Dowager attested to having the Eye of Dire Abbey on her person when she retired for the evening the only possible suspects were the aforementioned.

The first thing the Captain did, at the suggestion of green-in-the-gills Franks, was have the entire ship searched top to bottom. A large though probably not surprising amount of contraband was found in the crew's quarters, as well as in the hold, among it two exotic pets (a sickly python and a sullen toucan), several risqué Parisian postcards, four bottles of the Captain's best Merlot and a young female stowaway named Jeff who was sent to the galley to work off her/his passage. The Captain insisted his cabin be included in the search. In fact, due to the severity of the crime, only two passengers put up any fuss about the invasion of privacy.

Julia protested loudly, even fainting twice during the search (both times, conveniently, onto her pillow-covered bed). When the Bursar found several pieces of the Dowager's jewelry (but not the missing ruby), Julia explained that she was "saving them for safe-keeping." The Dowager had not reported the items as missing and dismissed the incident as "a household matter."

Mr. Jenks refused outright to allow a search of his cabin. When he finally relented, they found a dagger, a pistol, a derringer, a dagger, twenty bars of chocolate, four cartons of Lucky Strikes, a dagger and a dozen pairs of nylon stockings; in other words, the standard smuggler kit. Franks, watching through a porthole between visits to the railing, insisted they thoroughly check his luggage. In a hidden pocket on the side of Mr. Jenks' valise they discovered (in addition to a dagger) a diary full of seemingly random characters. The Bursar held it up to the porthole, but Franks could make no sense of what was obviously a code. Nevertheless, since the ruby had not turned up elsewhere, the man became to Franks the prime suspect. The Captain disagreed.

"No, no. I think we can scratch Mr. Jenks off the list," he said.

The Captain made this remark when Franks visited him on the fifth morning at sea. He seemed startled at the visit, quickly folding up the sheet of paper he had been studying.

"The jewel was not in his cabin."

"Exactly! He's a smuggler. He knows how to hide things."

Franks shook out his new putty Mackintosh. Despite the storm they had run into that morning, he suddenly felt wonderful. He had risen early, shaved without incident and finished off a cyclopean breakfast all before 7 a.m.

"So does that maid, Julia," the Captain said. He sniffed derisively. "Theater people."

"But Julia doesn't write in code. Even if he isn't a thief, this Jenks could be a spy for the Germans or Italians."

"My boy, we aren't at war. Not yet."

"At the very least, you should not let anyone off the ship until the jewel is found. We arrive soon at St. Helena. Anyone disembarking must be thoroughly searched.

"Agreed," the Captain said shortly.

Franks waited. The Captain would not look him in the eye; never a good sign. Franks brushed a piece of lint off his pant leg and waited some more. Finally, the Captain rose and grabbed a book from the bookcase.

"If you'll excuse me, Bernie, I have some important reading to do regarding..." He turned the book right side up. "'Emergency Veterinary Procedures.'"

"It's that Jenks fellow, obviously," the Count said, unsolicited.

After talking to the Captain, Franks had retired to the lounge. Anxious for some solitude, he instead found a packed house.

"But the Captain won't listen," the Count said, smoking angrily.

It seemed that everyone knew who did it; they only differed on the who. Knowing Franks was semi-officially on the case—and being trapped inside by the weather—virtually all the first-class passengers gathered around him to discuss it. After a few moments of polite listening, he excused himself.

Franks locked his fingers around the railing, not from dizziness but merely to keep from being blown overboard. The wind howled. The *Neuralgia* pitched ominously. He felt fantastic.

Watching a tern flying backwards, he pondered the case. The Captain was hiding something about Mr. Jenks—but what? Plus, the man had been up that night, had even stumbled into Franks' cabin.

"Mr. Franks?"

It was Gertrude, the German student. Even covered head to toe in a rain yellow parka, he still recognized her large, not unattractive proboscis.

"Miss von Kapukt. Don't tell me you also enjoy a good tempest?"

The tern slammed sideways into the forecastle, fell to the deck, shook its head vigorously and decided to take the day off.

"I've been looking for you," Gertrude shouted over the storm. I-I was wondering if you'd like some tea?"

They retired to the lounge. Franks had a tea, no sugar. Gertrude had black coffee. The room rolled viciously.

"I was wondering if I could show you something in my room," she said, balancing her cup. Her face reddened. "No—I don't mean—"

"Of course not!"

"It involves—well, it's silly. Forget I asked."

"No, please." Franks had enjoyed their earlier conversations. She was brilliant and fairly beautiful. In fact, were it not for her weak eyes and shovel nose she would have been striking. Out of his league, really. "What were you going to ask?"

"It's about Mr. Jenks. I think he's spying on me."

"See? The coffee tins have been rearranged."

They were in Gertrude's state room. Three tins of Uncle Puddly's Northumberland Premium Roast sat side by side on the small table.

Franks said nothing; his attention was drawn to the lace slip draped over a chair. *Those are girl things!* his mind shouted. He didn't get out much at university.

"Of course. You don't see," Gertrude said apologetically, simultaneously stuffing the unmentionable into a drawer. "But when I was last in the room, those tins were stacked in a triangle."

"Well, it's—" He was imagining the lace slip on Gertrude's tall, pale body. "The storm. They could have moved."

"It's possible. But also, my toiletries have been moved. I'm very particular about how I arrange them."

"You think someone entered your room last night." He pictured her strawberry blonde hair cascading as she released it from its customary tight bun.

"I think Mr. Jenks is following me. He always seems to show up wherever I am."

"Not unusual on a ship."

She touched his hand. "I'm not a silly school girl; I'm a mature woman."

"Yes. I see. I mean, I understand."

"You are a detective. I was wondering if you could keep your eye on that man."

"Yes. I will. Of course. Yes."

Then he was in the hallway, alone. *She touched me,* he thought. According to a book he once read, that meant a girl liked you.

Dinner at the Captain's table was an unpleasant one. The Count was upset because Mr. Jenks wasn't in the brig. Mr. Jenks was annoyed by what he termed an unreasonable room search. And the Captain said only three words to Franks all evening: "Pass the chutney." The Dowager's change in behavior was the most dramatic. No longer boisterous and exuberant, she had become quiet and melancholy. Perhaps mindful of her great loss, she now covered her ample bosom with conservative high-buttoned tops. Her appetite, though, remained healthy.

Franks was now working two cases, and noticed that as soon as Gertrude excused herself, Mr. Jenks did likewise. He followed them both. Gertrude made her way down the hall to the library. Jenks, although never looking at her, followed the same path. Gertrude eased herself into a comfy chair and started reading Nietzsche. Jenks, after browsing a shelf opposite her, turned and left.

After fifteen seconds had passed, Gertrude asked without looking up, "Is he gone?"

"Yes," Franks said, taking a seat nearby.

"He is following me, then?"

"Possibly." Away from the intimacy of her cabin, Franks was able to think more clearly. Jenks was certainly the most suspicious person onboard, but so what? And what would he want from Gertrude? A few tins of lousy English coffee?

"I'll keep an eye on him, but be careful. He could be dangerous."

"I am not without protection," she admitted. "I have a gun."

"A gun?"

"A luger. A gift from my uncle. He's the one I'm going to visit in East Africa. Actually, the coffee is for him."

"A gun is no good if you don't know how to use it."

"Oh, I'm an excellent shot. I placed first in the Heidelberg shooting tournament."

This put Franks' mind at ease, at least enough to allow it to focus on the missing jewels. He took a stroll on deck to sort things out. The ship still pitched, but stars were showing through the clouds.

"Odd," he said to no one, although the ship-bound tern seemed willing to listen. "Where does one hide a ruby? And who?"

Perhaps Julia had taken it. The Count had motive, but so did anyone who had seen the jewel, which was everyone.

But there was no getting around it—Mr. Jenks had to be the culprit.

"What do you think?" he asked the tern.

It shook out its wings and flew off. Franks watched it, a blotch of gray shrinking into the night sky. The clouds were almost gone. The stars were out. The sea was quickly flattening. Franks' stomach lurched.

At least he had solved one mystery—what made him seasick was calm water.

DEATH ON THE HIGH SEAS

Whoosh! Splash!

The weather report for their current location off the Iberian Peninsula called for clear skies. Franks was therefore pleasantly surprised to awaken to the sounds of high winds and waves breaking on his porthole.

Hhhhh-whoooo!

Who would have thought one could get seasick only on a calm sea? He had mentioned it to the Captain the previous night, but the veteran seaman had never heard of such a thing.

Creeeeak!

It was true, though. After a night of still waters and nausea, he felt fit as a fiddle with the morning storm.

Splash!

So fit in fact that when he arose the floor felt completely steady underneath him.

Knock, knock, knock.

"Mr. Franks, sir?"

Franks brushed back his hair, donned his robe and opened the door.

"Bursar Harrell, sir. Sorry to bother you so early, sir. But the Captain—" He paused. Someone outside whispered something. "Sorry to bother you what with this wicked storm and all, sir, but the Captain needs you in the hold."

Franks raised a questioning eyebrow.

"There's been a death, sir."

The words banished all grogginess from Franks. "Tell him I'll be down presently."

"Sorry, sir. The Captain asked us to escort you down immediately. Uh," (more whispering) "while the crime scene is fresh."

"Here he comes," the Captain hissed to the others in the ship's hold. "You all know the plan—ah, Mr. Franks. Thank heaven you're here."

Bernie Franks, having hastily added pants and slippers to his attire, viewed the scene. In the back of the hold, in an aisle formed by roped and battened-down trunks and crates, lay the body of Mr. Jenks.

The man's upper back and head were wedged against the bulkhead. There was blood on his shirt front, and a small pool on the floor near his right knee, which was bent at an unwholesome angle.

"Who found him?" Franks glanced around at the Captain, Bursar and two yeomen. They swayed rhythmically.

"Bursar Harrell here," the Captain said. "Swears he didn't touch anything. Came straight to me. Er, how's the seasickness?"

"Better, thanks to the storm."

As if on cue, the howls of gale-force winds increased. Franks thought he could actually make out the word "howl" in the cacophony.

"Oh, it's a fierce one," a crewman said, nodding to the Captain.

"Hard to stay steady even for us experienced seamen," another piped. "Yet you seem steady as a ship of the line, Mr. Franks."

Franks humbly shrugged off the compliment. Yet he did seem to be the only one not leaning from one side to the other.

Carefully, he bent over the body. It was not the first dead body he had encountered; he had, after all, been on several adventures with his father. But those deaths were usually disease or frostbite or crocodile-related. His was his first homicide. Uncertain, he felt Jenks' wrist.

"How long has he been dead?" the Captain asked.

"I'd say since he was shot." He dropped the wrist and examined the rest of the torso. "I see at least three entry wounds at the right knee, left biceps and chest. I—has the storm stopped?"

Franks had turned to address the others and noticed they had stopped swaying.

"Er..." said one.

"Um," said another.

"Calm before the storm," said the first hastily.

"Yes—sometimes the calm before the storm comes during the storm," added the other.

"I think it's picking up again," the Captain said loudly. "Yes. Definitely picking up!"

The howling resumed and the men began swaying, although it took them a moment to coordinate their movements.

Franks frowned. The crew had been acting oddly ever since they came for him. He wasn't familiar with every deck of the *Neuralgia*, but it seemed they had taken a circuitous route to the hold, always near the exterior but never on the outside. The storm seemed to be rolling in from all sides. The wind howled at every turn and water assaulted every porthole he passed. He saw no passengers, but the passageways were full of crew, all of whom were having trouble keeping their balance but still talkative enough to make a comment on the sudden storm.

Regardless, he had work to do.

"What do you make of that?" the Captain asked.

Frank looked. Lying next to the body, near a now-open hidden compartment of a steamer trunk, was a tin of Uncle Puddly's Northumberland Premium Roast.

"That is Mr. Jenks' trunk?"

"It is," the Captain replied.

"Why would he...?"

"There is something else." The Captain pointed back down the aisle.

About ten feet away was a gun. Franks took out his handkerchief and picked it up.

A luger.

Gertrude's luger!

Franks wandered away, perplexed. None of it made any sense, least of all the idea that the lovely, shovel-nosed Gertrude would shoot someone.

He felt queasy. The howling had stopped. The crew had ceased their swaying. He drew a curtain on a nearby porthole. It was calm and sunny; not a cloud to be seen. He opened a floral valise and dry-heaved.

The Captain looked sternly at the crew. "Honestly men, you call that fake swaying? And I want to know which one of those scallywags on wind duty actually said *howl!*"

The *RMS Neuralgia* arrived at St. Helena only a day behind schedule. The six passengers who disembarked were thoroughly searched under the Captain's watchful eye, as was their luggage. No one else was allowed to leave, disappointing those who wanted to see Longwood House, where Napoleon had spent his final years.

"Lady Pense ain't gonna like this," Julia complained when told of the order.

"It is for her own good," the Captain explained. We have tightened security so the jewel does not leave the ship. And now we have a murder to contend with.

"What about the crew? You suspect them, right?"

"The crew is not allowed to leave, either. All supplies are being carried to the ship and transferred to our crew under my supervision.

"Well, she ain't gonna like this," Julia repeated.

An hour after their first conversation, Julia approached the Captain again.

"Her highness wants cough drops for her laryngitis."

"Certainly," the Captain said.

"She needs ten boxes."

"Ten boxes!?"

"You're right," Julia mused. "Better make it twenty."

"I've something to tell you," the Captain said.

He and Franks were standing on the dock, close enough to the *Neuralgia* to watch the loading, yet far enough away for some privacy.

"It's about Mr. Jenks."

Franks breathed deeply. There was no seasickness on land at least.

"No. I have something to tell *you* about Mr. Jenks. He was out of his cabin the night of the theft. At the very least, he was snooping around Ms. von Kaputt's cabin.

"Very possibly!" the Captain said, suddenly irritated. "He was also in the Lady Pense's room."

Franks was stunned. "You're just telling me this now?" He thought about the ramifications. "Why isn't he under arrest?"

The Captain turned quickly from annoyance to remorsefulness. "He is, he was—well, read this." He unfolded a piece of paper and handed it to Franks.

"It's a coded message from the Admiralty's office. Received a few days ago."

ATTN, CAPTAIN, RMS NEURALGIA. PSNGR JENKS IS BRIT. INTELLIGENCE. PROVIDE ALL ASSISTANCE. TRACKING GERMAN AGENT.

Franks returned it. "This is the message you were reading when I barged in that morning?"

The Captain nodded.

"This explains your defense of Jenks, and your silence toward me."

"And leaves us no real suspects in theft of the Eye of Voir Dire Abbey."

"But—who killed him?"

They watched as the last of the items were carried up the gangplank: the cartons of lozenges, along with and a chafing dish and two cans of Sterno for the preparing what the Dowager had called an "old family recipe."

"This German agent, obviously."

Franks thought of Gertrude. "Yes. Obviously."

Two days into the second leg of their voyage, Bernard Franks was troubled. Not by the seas, which were comfortably choppy, but by his talks with Gertrude.

Yes, she admitted, it was her luger. Yes, she had confronted Mr. Jenks after he took one of her tins the night of the shooting. Pretending to stay asleep after he entered her room, she had followed him to the hold and found him putting the coffee tin in the secret compartment of his trunk.

"I brought the gun, for protection," she had told him as they talked quietly in her room earlier that day. "But I did not use it. I—I could not use it on a person."

"Still, it looks bad," Frank had said, patting her strong, pale hand. "It's your gun. It was fired several times; there were bullet holes in a six-foot radius around Jenks. And your fingerprints are all over it."

And you're German. He didn't say that at the time, but he was thinking it now. There was a German spy on the ship, and he or she had almost certainly shot Jenks, the British spy.

He walked the deck, deep in thought, but no answer came to him. And suddenly it was late afternoon. There was no alternative—he would have to turn Gertrude in to the Captain. The dinner bell rang. Looking up, he realized with dread that the storm had passed. His stomach did a jig.

Franks wobbled toward the Captain's cabin, hoping to catch him before the meal. On his way, he passed the Count and the Dowager, who were shooting skeet.

"Ugh, Count," the Dowager rasped, despite her sore throat. You couldn't hit a barn with a brick."

The Count sniffed. "What I lack in accuracy I make up for in persistence."

Franks found the Captain and quickly but reluctantly told him about Gertrude. After dinner, she was confined to her cabin and a guard placed outside. Bernie tried to visit her a few days later, but she refused to see him. Which was understandable.

UNCLE PUDDLY'S NORTHUMBERLAND PREMUIM ROAST

"Craziest thing I ever heard of," the Dowager commented. It was evening. The *Neuralgia* was just a few days out from Cape Town. She was playing cards with her entourage, wrapped to the neck due to her sore throat but otherwise in good spirits.

"It's true," Franks gasped. "Calm seas make me sick."

The weather had been miserably wonderful.

"Very strange," she said as she dealt.

"I'd be more worried about recovering our jewel if I were you." That was the Count. "I can't believe Jenks didn't have it."

"Let's just hope it turns up," the Dowager said.

"Captain says nobody's leaving the ship until it's found," Julia said. The Dowager's maid was the new fourth now that Jenks had retired from the game.

"At least your throat is improving," the Count said.

"It comes and goes," the Dowager said, suddenly in a whisper. "Which reminds me Julia–shouldn't we be whipping up that family recipe?"

"Sure, your highness."

"Excuse us." The Dowager rose. "I hope your feel better, Mr. Franks."

Franks nodded his head, which was already hanging low.

"I'm wondering," the Dowager continued in a stage whisper. "Seasickness is like stage fright. And there's a tried and true cure for that, right Julia?"

"Mmm hmm," Julia agreed.

Franks looked at the Dowager, sick and cynical. She handed him a bottle of off-brand whiskey.

"Drink up."

Franks remembered the rest of that night in bits and pieces. A nearly-full bottle. Singing bawdy lyrics with Julia. A half-full bottle. Demonstrating, with the Dowager's assistance, a wedding dance he had learned from the Inuit. A quarter-full bottle. Putting the Count in a sleeper hold. An empty bottle. Lying on his bed, idly turning the tin of Uncle Puddly's Northumberland Premium Roast and thinking, *Why would anyone bring English coffee to East Africa when you can get the good stuff in any market?* A broken bottle. Wondering if Gertrude were indeed a spy and hating himself for thinking it. Pondering who took the Eye of Voir Dire Abbey and where they could hide it. Thinking about the Dowager's cleavage uncovered and covered.

He awoke the next morning with a hangover, his sea legs, an empty coffee tin and all the answers.

After breakfast, a day out from Cape Town, the Dowager, Julia and the Count were brought to the lounge.

"We have searched the ship stem to stern and found nothing," Franks told the assembled group. "The next step, as regrettable as it may be, is to search each person's, um, person."

"A body search?" the Count spat. "I must object."

His scowl was matched by Julia's.

"Oh no you ain't," she said.

Franks looked to the Captain, who nodded his approval.

"Now, now. I know this is irregular, but the Captain believes it is justified due to the importance of retrieving the jewel."

"But–" the Count said.

Frank held up a hand to stop him.

"The Captain is also asking, as a demonstration of good faith, that the Dowager subject herself to the same search."

Now it was the Dowager's turn to scowl. She placed a hand on her breast, currently covered by high-button velvet blouse and a silk scarf, and opened her mouth to speak–but stopped abruptly. Julia had caught her eye and given her a quick nod. The Dowager composed herself.

"I reckon," she said finally, "I've been subjected to worse in my New York days. If it will solve the case I'll do it."

"Thank you," Franks said.

"I only have one condition–that I be allowed to freshen up."

Franks crinkled his brow and threw a questioning glance at the Captain.

"Begging your pardon, your ladyship," the Captain said. "I hope you realize that a member of the crew–female in the case of you and your maid–will have to remain with you."

"Even in the privy?" the Count asked.

"No. Not in the privy, obviously. But the privies will be searched. The thoroughness is regrettable but necessary."

They reconvened after breakfast, escorted by their appointed crew members. While they dined their cabins were searched. Franks had insisted they include the Dowager's quarters "for fairness' sake." The jewel was not found.

The plan was for each of the three to enter the second room one at a time and disrobe. They and their clothes would then be searched by crew members.

The Dowager, who seemed to be in a better mood, nudged the Count in the ribs. "Well, County, I guess we know who done it now. Process of elimination and the like."

The Count pouted and said nothing.

"Well—who's first?" Frank asked.

The trio looked one to the other.

"Shucks. May as well get it over with," Julia said and marched into the other room, followed by a laundry maid and a female cook.

Franks took a seat. "Now we wait."

Ten minutes later the women emerged. The linen maid shook her head to indicate she had found nothing.

Franks did not look surprised. Neither did the Dowager. The Count leaped to his feet.

"This is ridiculous waste of time! It was the Jenks fellow. The smuggler."

"Now Count," the Captain said. "My people have searched everywhere."

"Yeah County," the Dowager said with satisfaction. "It's all fair and square. Now get in there and strip."

The Count backed away from the others, looking desperately about. "But, but—it's impossible. Wait! What about that German girl? The murderess?"

"She and her belongings have also been searched," the Captain said.

"Please, Count," Franks said calmly. "Go into the next room. The Bursar is waiting. Her ladyship has consented to the same treatment, isn't that right, Your Ladyship?"

She winked. "Always up for a bit of fun."

After huffing and puffing, the Count exited to the other room. Franks turned to the Dowager.

"Chilly, Lady Pence?"

She smiled sweetly. "The sea breeze, I reckon. The laryngitis."

"To be sure."

Franks did not take his eyes off the Dowager until the door opened.

"Captain. Mr. Franks. Will you come in here please?" It was the Bursar.

Inside they found the Count, fully dressed except for his jacket, which was held in one hand of the Bursar. In the other was the Eye of Dire Abbey.

"It was right there in his inside pocket, Captain."

"I knew it!"

The Dowager stood at the door, Julia just behind her.

"Makes perfect sense, when you think about it. He's always been jealous that the estate went to me. In fact, it would have if he would have gotten all three of us in the so-called croquet accident."

The Count, who had been crestfallen, lifted his head, his face full of hatred.

"That is a damnable lie, you—you commoner! Traipsing around half-naked, showing off our family's jewel for anyone to steal! You've ruined the family name and its fortune. Ruined it!"

"Says the man with the stolen ruby," she said calmly.

"For shame!" Julia added. "I knew he was bad, I just didn't think he would stoop this low."

The Captain signaled to the Bursar, who opened the other door to let in two armed crewmen.

"Count du Compte, I am placing you under arrest. Take him to the brig."

The Count was dragged away, proclaiming his innocence all the way down the passageway. Meanwhile, Juia had returned with a jewelry box and placed the gem inside.

"Lady Pence," the Captain continued. "I must insist on keeping the Eye in my personal safe until we disembark tomorrow in Cape Town."

The Dowager nodded. "I'll go along with that. Thank you so much for recovering the thing. You too, Mr. Franks."

Franks mumbled a reply.

"I knew if we put our heads together we could pull it off," the Captain said.

Bernie Franks stared out the porthole of the Captain's study. The water was azure but choppy. Fat clouds hurried across the bright blue sky. He wouldn't be needing that whiskey today. On the other side of the ship, the port side, passengers could no doubt see the port of Cape Town coming into view, with the sheer cliffs of Table Mountain forming a dramatic backdrop. It was their last day at sea. They would disembark in four hours.

Franks should have been packing, since he had to catch another ship that evening to the East African city of Dar-as-Salaam' where he would join his father, Major Wendell Franks (Ret.). He should have been proud to have solved his first major case. Instead, he was brooding.

"Quit your sulking, boy! We did it. Solved a murder, captured a spy and recovered a jewel. Like Holmes and Watson."

Franks punched the bulkhead a little harder than he intended. A jolt of pain shot clear up to the elbow.

"But I was wrong. I was wrong about who did it."

"Don't be so hard on yourself. You narrowed it down to two suspects. So what if you guessed the wrong one?" The Captain stood up and straightened a few books in the case. "I wouldn't be surprised if there were a commendation in this for you. Maybe a monetary reward from Lady Pence."

Franks cradled his sore hand and said nothing.

"A singular woman, the Dowager," the Captain continued. "Having to go through such an adventure. Yet she seems unfazed by it all. Saw her on deck and she was happy as a clam. Mind you, she still has a bit of a throat—bundled up like my granny."

"Must be disappointing for her," Franks admitted. "She loves to show off her, um, assets."

"Quite a case of laryngitis, surely. Do you know she used up all the cough drops we took on at St. Helena?"

"Huh," Franks said. He flexed his hand. The middle finger was starting to swell.

"Pity too," the Captain continued. "Had a bit of a tickle myself this morning and there wasn't a lozenge to be found."

Franks pulled on the affected finger and immediately regretted it.

"My favorite flavor, too. Cherry."

Franks turned quickly, the pain forgotten.

"Cherry. Did you say cherry?"

"Yes. Cherry cough drops. She used them all up."

The Count was in the brig, slumped against the wall. The door opened. He scowled.

"What do you want?"

"If you confess to what you *did* do," Franks said, "I'll clear you of what you *didn't* do."

GUILTY AND
INNOCENT AND GUILTY

"I'm free? Really?"

"I turned you in but I never doubted you."

Gertrude rushed up to Franks. She stopped short of hugging him, squeezed his forearm instead.

"But how?"

"The Count confessed to shooting Mr. Jenks. He had been going to the hold every night since the jewel disappeared on the hunch that Jenks would stash it there again after the luggage had been searched. When he saw the man hiding something in that hidden compartment, he confronted him. They wrestled. The count found your luger on the floor and shot Jenks."

"But—how did you know it wasn't me?" She batted her weak eyes at him.

"I was pretty sure." He was distracted by her watery eyes. "You're a good shot. You told me. The count is a bad shot. Based on the number and wildness of the shots, Jenks was killed by a bad shot."

"Yes. I doubt I could miss at that distance. But I could not shoot anything living."

They sat down in her room.

"So the Count took the jewel from Jenks."

Franks laughed. It was a horsy noise and not his best trait. "We shall see."

The Dowager and her maid stood on the main deck, next to their luggage. The *Neuralgia* had docked and the two were first in line, waiting for the gangplank to be set in place.

"Aren't you forgetting something, your Ladyship?"

Franks stood next to the Captain, who was holding up the Eye of Dire Abbey.

Both the Dowager and Julia seemed flustered when they saw the ruby.

"Oh! Of course. How could I forget it?" Lady Pence said. "Must be all the drama of the voyage."

She reached out to take the jewel, but Franks grabbed it first.

"So this is the famous Eye of Dire Abbey," Franks said, holding it up. "This is the first time I've given it a good look since I saw you wearing it that first night out."

"Yes," the Dowager said, a bit anxiously.

"I wonder how it tastes?"

"No!" the Dowager cried.

Franks licked the ruby. And then, to the horror of everyone, he bit down on it. Remarkably, a jagged corner came off in his mouth. He chewed thoughtfully.

"Mmmm. Cherry."

The Captain stared, mouth hanging open. "You just bit a priceless gem."

"No. The Eye of Dire Abbey is quite intact, is it not, your Ladyship?"

The Dowager sighed deeply and smiled. Then she unbuttoned her blouse and removed the real Eye of Dire Abbey from her cleavage.

"How did you know?" she asked.

"I didn't. Not until I remembered the cherry lozenges."

"I don't understand," the Captain said. "She stole her own ruby? Why?"

"My guess," Franks said to Lady Pence, "was that you wanted to escape the life of the gentry. Per our earlier conversation."

The Dowager turned, letting the breeze cool her newly exposed neck. "Gosh darn bore! Everybody fretting about how I behave. And that greedy Count watching every penny I spend. I figured me and Julia would disappear. I sell the ruby and she could sell the jewelry you found in her cabin."

"Amazing," the Captain said.

"What I don't understand is why you decided to frame Count du Compte."

"Ha!" Julia said. "That was my idea. Wasn't even part of the plan to start with. At first we was just going to run off. With that ruby gone the estate would revert to the King and the Count wouldn't have nothing anyway. But then you and the Captain wouldn't stop snooping around and it was looking like no one would be able to leave the boat until the Eye turned up. And her Ladyship was already playing the laryngitis role–"

"Then we got that steaming tray and the cough drops and made our own ruby," the Dowager said. "We used to make costume jewelry out of all kinds of stuff back in our burlesque days."

The Captain, being a bit slow on the best of days, was having trouble following the explanation. "But that's–but how could you hope to pass it off a giant cough drop as the real thing?"

"Well, we didn't know if we would even need the fake one," the Dowager continued. "At worst we figured we'd drop it somewhere on the ship a few hours before reaching Cape Town and slip away with the real one before anyone was the wiser." She sat down on a steamer trunk. "But when you cooked up that body search scheme I was glad Julia had thought of a backup plan. I just had to delay the search a bit.

Back in the cabin I pocketed the cough drop ruby when that linen maid's back was turned and slipped it into the Count's pocket when I jabbed him in the ribs."

"And you would have let him take the blame for the crime," the Captain noted.

"Why not? I figure he was the one who set up that croquet accident. He would have inherited everything if I hadn't have stepped away at the right moment."

"But you did," Franks said slowly. "And because you did, you were the one who inherited everything. But that who-done-it will have to await another sleuth."

"One thing I don't understand," Gertrude said.

She and Franks were awaiting the ship to Dar es Salaam and after spending the day together in Cape Town, holding hands and discussing Planck's Constant. "Why did Jenks steal my uncle's coffee?"

"I wondered about that as well. Did I tell you Mr. Jenks was a British agent? He was searching for a Nazi spy, and with you being German..."

Gertrude adjusted her glasses. "But why the coffee?"

"Gertrude," he said. *What a lovely name!* "There was no spy. The coffee tin itself was the spy."

Her eyes widened to less of a squint than usual.

"I was fiddling with the tin and it opened. Hidden inside were copies of British military plans for East Africa. Numbers, troop placements, etcetera. I gave them to the Captain to dispose of."

Gertrude said nothing, just looked at his neck. "You've got a smudge on your collar," she said at last.

Bernard tried unsuccessfully to brush it off.

"Well, I guess a little dirt won't harm me."

EINSTEIN'S THEORIES

Well, that was the first case I've written up for the doc, just like Dr. Watson did for Sherlock Holmes. Except the doc's the doctor and I'm just a guy everybody thinks isn't too smart.

I'm Einstein, by the way. And I guess I should say I'm typing up the cases not writing them because I'm taking a typing class at the Tribeca YMCA. I'm up to thirty words per minute. Pretty good, right? Of course I missed the day we learned the upper row so I have to look when I type numbers or little symbols like @, ^, $, * and %. But you don't use those much. I wish I were better with the numbers, though. I should say numerals 'cause did you know they call numbers numerals? So I gave him the story and maybe he'll read it before I go on vacation. I'm going to Florida in a few weeks. How 'bout that?

When I say I'm the doctor's assistant I should say it's only when he has a case and when he lets me assist. Like with serving the coffee. And when I'm not busy with my newsstand. And when *Lawrence Welk* isn't on. Not that I'm in love with Lawrence Welk or anything. I'm more of a Myron Floren man. Sometimes I drive him places. The doc, not Myron Floren. He had a nice car once–the doc, I mean. Saved up a long time for it. But it turned out to be a lemon. Blew a rod with only a hundred miles on it, right there on the bridge from Manhattan to Staten Island. That's what you get for buying from Dinky Dave Ford. Never trust a TV car guy, I say. But whether he asks me or not I always keep an eye on him. He's a really smart guy but he needs looking after.

I work hard at the newsstand, but it's only for seven hours a day. But it's seven days a week, rain or shine, summer and winter. Except when I'm on a vacation, like I will be in December. Guess where I'm going? Florida. I own my newsstand. Know why? My dad gave it to me. He's been dead for four years. I make a good living too. Know why? I don't gamble or drink or fool around with women. "Never gamble or drink or fool around with women," my dad used to tell me, and he knew what he was talking about because he did all three. Most newsstand guys (and gals—there's at least two I know of) are broke because they play the ponies or drink, and a few are hooked on heroin and stuff. Not me. My dad raised me better. I do chew gum, though. Know what brand? Teaberry.

Anyway, the doc was pretty low after blowing the Midget Murder Spree case. I don't blame Dr. Franks for blowing this case. From what I hear that police inspector backed him into a corner. But you'd be amazed—I've seen the doc solve cases with less evidence than he had in this one. Like the Case of the Itchy Loud Thing, for instance, where he made a mad count confess merely by opening a bottle of Yoo-Hoo. And in Dr. Franks Gets a Clue he tricked the widow into revealing damning evidence just by mispronouncing the word *methane*. Not that the doc names his cases. I figure that's my job. Someday, when I retire from selling papers I'm going to write them all up and then he'll be famous. I already typed one up and gave it to him, like I said. I'm taking a typing class at the Y. But he's probably too down to read it any time soon.

But boy! This case, which I'm thinking of calling Dr. Franks and the Antmen, was a real toughie. And for the doc to be humiliated like that—in his own mother's basement no less—

well, he took it pretty hard. For one thing, he was counting on the homoscience money to get his own place.

When he stopped by my newsstand that Saturday morning he barely said shut up, which is how he greets me. I'll say something like, "Hey doc, it's a great day, isn't it?" and before I can even finish he'll say "Shut up, Einstein." But this time he talked so low I wasn't sure what he said. He was so down in the dumps he didn't even bother to point out typographical errors on the dailies. And he barely grunted when he saw the top story about a circus midget who died wrestling an elephant. *Little men dying? No thank you,* he said. Then he dropped the morning papers in his A&P bag. The good one with the twine handles. I saw three Entenmann's coffee cakes and a half gallon of chocolate milk in the bag. That could only mean the doc was going on a bender because his mother doesn't like pastries. And it was only eight in the morning. I watched him walk off down Lexington, kind of dragging his feet, on past the Guggenheim, heading for home and a sugar high.

At least Stella helped him. Did I tell you about Stella? She's a real pip, as my dad used to say. Reminds me of one of the Lemmon Sisters only bigger and in a waitress outfit. Have you seen the Lemmon Sisters on *Lawrence Welk?* They're pretty. Prettier than Lawrence and Myron Floren put together.

But Stella was later. This was just the weekend after doc got tossed off the case. November. Next month I'm going on vacation. Guess where. Florida. How 'bout that?

The rest of that day, Saturday, I didn't see Doc at all. Sunday neither. I think his mother picks up a *Sunday Times* after mass so he didn't really need to go out. I'm sure he'll be okay. If anybody can eat that much coffee cake and chocolate milk and survive it's the doc.

Monday he had lunch with Cousin Phelps. Not at Wang's though because Wang's is closed for remodeling because Stella owns it now. Which is a new thing.

I don't know if you know Phelpsy. He's a nice enough guy, but a little shifty if you catch my drift. Always wears nice clothes but never has any money. Definitely not the kind of guy you want handling your finances. But he did go to school to be an accountant, and he is Mrs. Franks' sister's son, so the doc is kind of stuck with him.

So they went to Hamburger Heaven over on Lexington and Concord. I hear they discussed the doc's long-awaited royalty check. Phelpsy finally owned up that he had invested the money in a thoroughbred. I happen to have seen the nag and it could only be called a racehorse because it has four legs and a tail. I don't gamble, like I said, but sometimes I go to the track with the other news guys just to watch.

Anyway, Phelpsy also said he'd set up some meetings that week for the doc to pitch inventions to some big companies. He's always got some great new gizmo on the drawing board. So at least the doc would be getting out of the house.

I should also explain about Dr. Franks and the electric can opener. It's true he didn't really invent the can opener part. But the invention didn't become a big seller until he came up with the knife sharpener thingie on the back. And he's invented lots of other things as well. They just tend to be ahead of their time. At least that's what he tells me.

Tuesday when he stopped by the newsstand to pick up his *Mad* magazine he seemed like he was in a slightly better mood, even though one of his fingers was bandaged from where that obese squirrel bit him (obese–I read that word in one of the journals I sell). Doc said he had a big "pitch meeting" at the Waldorf with some bigwigs from General Motors. He was even chipper enough to point out a few grammatical errors in the Post.

"New missing persons case?" he said in that classy English accent of his. It should be new missing *person* case."

I looked at the story and, sure enough, it was only about one guy. A toll booth operator who hadn't been heard from in a week. It was one of a series of cases of missing persons, but when you're talking about one man I guess that's a missing person.

I'm getting most of this second-hand, but my sources are reliable. I hear a lot on the street and I am in the newspaper business even if I just sell them. The point is you can believe me when I tell you what happened that week, even though I didn't see the doc until Friday, which was the day of the library incident. Also, I've got it all written down somewhere. Did I mention I'm writing a book about all of the doc's cases? I'm taking a typing class and I practice every night except when *Lawrence Welk* is on.

He could see the nuts. They were right there inside the cave. Only now he couldn't get at them. He flicked his tail in agitation. Winter was coming and things were getting stupid.

He pushed against the hard air at the cave entrance. Usually if he angled toward the bottom he could work his way through and get at the big monster's big store of sweet, round, crunchy nuts. They were better than any nuts he had ever eaten. After eating the stupid monster's nuts he didn't want the others.

He slammed his head against the solid air with no effect. Stupid air! It made him crazy—the nuts were right there! He barked but it did no good. A stupid grackle landed nearby and he barked at that too until it hopped away. Then he turned back to look at those sweet, stupid nuts.

The last cold time was really stupid. It nearly killed him. His tail was thin and his rib cage was showing. Then in the middle of the warm times he found the nuts, and he ate and ate and what he didn't eat he buried for later. And the big stupid monster just let him take them.

But lately, just when he sensed the cold times were coming back, things were getting stupid again. The stupid ground was higher. It never used to scrape his belly when he ran, but now he had a bald spot on his stomach. And everything had gotten harder. The stupid branches were harder to chew. Even the sweet nuts bothered his stupid teeth (what few were left).

The stupidest thing was his tree. It had become slippery and it was harder and harder to climb. Often he would start climbing, only to slide down with a plop. The stupid plop was also new.

He leaned against the cave entrance. The stupid grackle was coming back, but he didn't have the energy to bark at it. At least the bird's presence meant there were no stupid cats around.

The big stupid monster wasn't in the cave and hadn't been for a few days, not since he bit it. Usually the big stupid monster would just sit on its haunches and do nothing while he took the nuts. That last time, though, it reached for him with its big, stupid, pink paws. He had no choice but to bite it with one of his remaining teeth. Were the two things connected—the bite and the stupid monster's absence? His stupid little squirrel brain didn't know.

The grackle hopped back over and pecked at him a few times, but he was still too tired to do anything about it. He looked back in the cave, which was dark and empty, except for the tasty nuts in the hollowed-out thing near the entrance. Where was the big stupid monster when he needed him? The grackle poked him in the stomach. Summoning the last of his energy, he barked and lurched at it until it flew off. That showed that stupid bird.

Only now his stupid chest hurt, and his left paw was numb. He leaned against the hard air that separated him from the cave.

Big stupid monster!

DR. DRIPLE

Stupid squirrel.

The bite looked slight enough—just a quarter-inch red line across the tip of the finger. Dr. Franks had cleaned it promptly and doused it with mercurochrome and had the optimistic thought that he wouldn't get rabies.

Satisfied, he rewrapped the finger and joined his mother in the living room. It was Sunday afternoon and she was watching *Thriller Suspense Theater. Dr. Jekyll and Mr. Hyde.*

"Sweet gravy, that's not an evil potion—it's hair tonic," the doctor said, spewing bits of raspberry coffee cake on the carpet. "Frederic March's hairline is clear down to his eyebrows."

"That nice." His mother was on the couch, tearing out coupons. "At least you're chipper enough to complain again. Like that time you said a real scientist would have clearly labeled Frankenstein's neck terminals 'positive' and 'negative.'"

"Hey, friends, this is Dinky Dave. The little man with the big deals."

"Dinky Dave?" Mrs. Franks said without looking up. "Isn't that the fellow you had all that trouble with a few years back?"

"Yes," Dr. Franks said quickly.

108

"The one who sold you that junker and you threatened to kill?"

Dr. Franks muttered a reply.

"And now you're not allowed within one hundred feet of him?"

"Yards. One hundred yards."

"Well, water under the bridge. Ooo! Spam's on sale!"

"...the little man with the big deals on brand new Fords!"

The camera followed Dinky Dave, sporting a wide pinstripe suit on his short, stocky frame, as he approached the auto.

"We've got two beautiful new models here at Dinky Dave Ford: the 1955 Crown Victoria and the lovely Henna."

The camera dollied out to reveal a two-tone car and a statuesque blonde, both rotating on a raised platform.

"Howdy, ya-all," squeaked Henna in what was possibly an attempt at a Southern drawl.

"Look at the sleek lines on that baby," Dinky Dave narrated. "And the car ain't bad either."

Dr. Franks' stomach bubbled. The chocolate milk was suddenly not setting well. And yet, he had to admit the Lovely Henna was aptly named. Tall, sleek and unnaturally blonde, with perfect features. Like an Amazonian Grace Kelly. And there was something familiar about her eyes.

"—tmen club. I'm not just the founder, but a satisfied customer. That's Dinky Dave—the little man with the big deals on Fords."

What was that about a club? Dr. Franks wondered what new scam Dinky Dave had concocted. "Maybe I'll just go back to bed."

"You've been sleeping all weekend. Besides, Cousin Phelps wants to meet you."

"Ugh. Not today."

"Yes, today—noon at Wang's Chop Suey or whatever you call it."

"You could have told me." He stood and brushed out his waistcoat.

"I did. Twice—ooo, five cents off chocolate chips. You just ignored me and pulled the covers over your head."

"Phelpsy should know Wang's is closed for the weekend. New ownership."

"Well. Whatever. Just go meet him.

Dr. Franks rose slowly, looking like a condemned man going for a stroll in the prison yard, and shuffled off to get his mac and hat.

"Maybe he has my can opener money."

"He's a good boy."

"He's a con artist."

"He's family."

A hunched, greasy-haired, hyperactive figure in an oversized black trench coat glided into Hamburger Heaven. His hands were jammed into his pockets and his small head seemed to be hiding between his shoulder blades. The man kept looking back behind him, as if he were being chased. But then Cousin Phelps always looked like that.

Seeing Dr. Franks, the man gave a quick nod and hurried over.

"Phelpsy."

Cousin Phelps slid into the booth, shrugged his shoulders a few times, looked quickly about, picked up the menu and glanced at it without actually reading it.

"What's up with Wang's? There's some dame in there scrubbing the floors like nobody's business."

"New owner."

Dr. Franks nodded. He had actually met the *dame*. She lent him a pen and paper so he could leave a note for Phelpsy, who had been late as usual. Her name was Stella. *Howdy, I'm Stella. What can I do for you, handsome?* A big woman—not fat but sturdily built. Red hair or maybe brown, hidden under a scarf.

She had been scrubbing the counter when he had arrived (who knew there was wood underneath the grime?). Shook his hand like a man. Told him to make sure to stop by on Monday. Called him hon.

Phelpsy turned the menu over a few times. "What do they got to eat here?"

"Hamburgers."

Noticing a rolled-up newspaper poking out of his cousin's breast pocket, Dr. Franks grabbed it. It was covered with handwritten scribbles.

"Freaking Dodgers are killing me," Phelps said.

"Phelpsy, a coin is fifty per cent accurate. It takes human intelligence," The doctor tapped him on the forehead with the paper, "to do worse than that."

Phelps looked down. "Freaking Dodgers."

The doctor got a cheeseburger. Phelps ordered hot water and ketchup. ("I'm trying to lose weight," he said, waving a bony arm.) Not a good omen. The cousins eyed each other. Phelps' pupils darted around like those of a cornered squirrel (a look the other knew only too well from recent experience).

"So…where are my royalties?"

Cousin Phelps fiddled with the sugar.

"It's complicated."

"Complicated? It's been three years. Federal Electric is selling millions of those can openers. They've even got them in designer colors. You're telling me they haven't cut me one check yet?"

When Dr. Franks sold the rights to his invention his mother had insisted he hire his cousin as a business partner. "He's an excellent bookkeeper," she had said. "He keeps several sets at a time."

"Funny you should mention that," Cousin Phelps said. He was looking down and carefully tearing the paper placemat into strips. "We did get a payment several months ago, but, being your business partner, I sort of reinvested it."

"Oh Lord! Not the dog track?"

"Don't be silly. This time it was a horse."

Dr. Franks felt a headache coming on. Part of him had long suspected he would never see any royalties, but the reality of it felt like heartbreak combined with a sucker punch—which was actually not far off the mark.

"And did they shoot our investment before or after the race?" he sighed.

"During, actually. It's a funny story—" He stopped, seeing the doctor's expression.

"So..., to sum up. You lost all my money on a dead horse."

Cousin Phelps' head bobbed from side to side. "Not all of it."

"Fine. Give me the rest. That will do for a start. Unless—"

Cousin Phelps shrugged defensively.

"Freaking Dodgers."

The food arrived. Phelps made a big deal of pouring ketchup into his hot water. With every slurp he would look shyly across the table.

"Can—can I have one of those fries?" he at last.

Dr. Franks pushed the plate across the table.

"Take it all, Phelpsy. Take it all."

Chirping and light.

Dr. Franks opened one eye, just a crack, and once he did he was wide awake, what with the damn sparrows making a racket and the low autumn sun in his face and the immediate return of that empty feeling in his solar plexus.

His mouth was sour and sticky. The upholstered electric chair (providentially unplugged yet still smelling of burnt suede) held his body like an oversized catcher's mitt. In his lap, miraculously untipped, a quart of chocolate milk. How many more quarts, he wondered, would it take to forget the past few days?

He stood up, knees cracking, vertebrae popping, and staggered to the window. After waiting for his bleary eyes to adjust to the light, he pushed it open and placed the melamine bowl outside. The doctor had decided not to risk another bite from Dash. The scratch on his hand seemed to be healing—or was that only wishful thinking brought about by a pathological fear of needles? The only thing that could make this week worse would be a painful series of rabies shots.

The basement door creaked.

"Bernie? Are you all right?"

His mother had obviously been waiting for him to get up. Dr. Franks ran a hand over his face.

"What time is it?"

"I was worried about you. Do you want some Wheatena?"

"Umph."

He lit a Turkish Dandy on his Bunsen burner and took a deep drag to clear his head. It was Monday. He checked his watch. 1:30 p.m. GMT—9:30 a.m. in his basement. So he hadn't been asleep that long. Twelve hours or so. Bad dreams, though. About his father, of course. They were in the Bengali jungle, which in the dream was right next to their current house. The great man was fighting off a tiger with a protractor and Bernie, just a young boy, was playing in the yard. "Bernard! I need those calculations," his father called. He was fending off the big cat with his forearm and slapping its head harmlessly with the protractor. Dr. Franks had always hated the way his father said his name: *BERN-urd.* Young Franks looked for his abacus, but suddenly the yard was filled with all the supplies and junk from his basement office. "Quick!" his father pleaded. "What's the force vector?" But young Bernard could not locate the abacus—or even a slide rule. All the while his father was pulled further and further into the underbrush. "Bern-urd, Bern-urd," he cried. Then silence.

Dr. Franks sat down in his broken office chair and took a swig of the chocolate milk. It was warm but okay. *Damn his father,* he thought. The great hunter and explorer. The absent father and husband.

He checked the window again. There was no sign of Dash—and these days the squirrel was hard to miss. Slowly, he released twin pensive streams of smoke through his nostrils. He had studied a bit of psychology as an undergraduate, and written one of his master's theses on electrostatic therapy (an experimental approach involving deep-pile carpet and metal work boots). Unresolved parental issues often interfered with success later in life. Perhaps, he mused, his recent bout of failure was somehow related to his father.

Cousin Phelps had brought one piece of good news. He had managed to set up not one but two meetings with established companies. With homoscience seemingly in the toilet, selling a product idea was his only way out of the basement. And for that, he would have to be in top form mentally—and psychologically.

He tamped out his fagot, putting it in his pocket for later. It was time to visit Dr. Driple.

"Mother," he called. "I'm off to see the shrink!"

"Pick up some flour. I'm making Tollhouse cookies for bridge club."

"So I hear you saying you blame mother."

Dr. Franks uttered a harrumph that many years of practice had made both convincing and onomatopoeic.

Dr. Harold ("call me Hal") Driple was not the best therapist in New York, but he was the only one the doctor could afford. Driple provided free sessions to Dr. Franks in exchange for lessons in hypnosis.

"My mother is a saint. She gave up a thrilling and successful life to raise me. If either of my parents shares any of the blame..."

"Yes?" Driple leaned forward, fingers steepled in front of him in what Dr. Franks recognized as the Carl Rogers active listening pose.

"Er, can you stop doing that? It's disingenuous."

Driple leaned back, rested his pointy chin on his fingers and nodded sympathetically.

"I hear you saying you have authority issues."

"When did you hear me say that?"

"Not in so many words."

Dr. Franks looked around Driple's office, taking in the familiar items: the African fertility statue with exaggerated breasts and stylized womb, the oil painting of geese taking flight, the leather-bound books that had not changed position in the three years.

"That's the problem. You're so busy trying to look like you're listening to me that I don't think you're actually listening."

Driple pursed his lips, leaned back into his wingback chair, smoothed out his argyle cardigan and looked the doctor in the eye.

"There," he said. "I'm sitting here. Listening. Now stop making excuses and tell me what's bothering you."

Dr. Franks bent forward, knees wide, eyes focused on a piece of lint on the mosaic rug. He lit a Turkish Dandy, took a long drag and held it before slowly exhaling the smoke through his nostrils.

"I've been thinking about the last time I saw dad."

DAR ES SALAAM

It was 1938 in what was then known as Tanganyika. Bernard Franks was disembarking at Dar es Salaam after a sea voyage from Tilbury by way of Capetown. Though he had traveled all over the world with his famous explorer father this was his first solo trip. His time aboard the *RMS Neuralgia* had been an eventful one. A storm overtook them near the Antilles, driving them hundreds of miles off course. Someone stole the jewelry of a buxom dowager (it was to be Bernard's first real case). Perhaps more notably he made the acquaintance of a fetching German undergraduate. Her name was Gertrude, a theology student at Heidelberg University with lifeless brown hair, weak gray eyes and the nose of a bottom-feeding shark. They spent many happy hours strolling about the ship and discussing the merits of redaction criticism and goat's milk. Alas, with war on the horizon a romance was not to be, which was just as well given Bernard's attitude toward goat's milk. All the same, he was disappointed when the ship arrived in Dar es Salaam and Gertrude was nowhere to be found; he had hoped at least for a lingering handshake.

Major Dr. Wendell Franks, OEE, PhD, DDS (Ret.), met his son at the pier. His first words, before hello or good to see you, were, "St. Anne's College, eh? Couldn't get into Magdalen?"

Bernard, all of eighteen, stammered a reply. "I thought just getting into Oxford was good enough."

Wendell looked up at his son, dark eyes barely visible beneath the rim of his pith helmet. Smaller and skinnier than Bernard had remembered but no less intimidating.

"Bah–St. Anne's." Then he pivoted quickly on his bandy little legs and marched off toward downtown Dar es Salaam. "Get your gear," he called back. "We're on a shed-ule."

Bernard stood frozen for an instant. He hadn't even had time to freshen up and give his hair a quick brushing, let alone take a quick look around in the hope of spying Gertrude. But this was typical Major Franks. Bernard grabbed his grip and canvas pack and hurried after his father.

It was not long before he had outpaced the older man. At the corner he flagged down an open-air carriage operated by a lethargic driver and a lifeless mule, but if Bernard thought his take-charge attitude would impress his father he was mistaken.

"What are you–made of money?" Wendell Franks asked as he jogged up. "We'll run to our destination. Stretch your legs a bit." Then he jogged off, casting nary a shadow in the noon-day sun.

Mad dogs and Englishmen, Bernard thought as he was again compelled to play catch up.

They were passing through the European section–tea shops and haufbrauhausen–dodging around the usual assortment of colonial Germans and Brits. Bernard, whose physical activity had lately been restricted to pacing the shelter deck after dinner, soon developed a stitch in his side and a cramp in his left leg–all the while juggling his luggage. But he wasn't going to give his father the satisfaction of seeing him give up. He gritted his teeth and doubled his pace as they passed into the more traditional part of town. A sheik stood in his way–he dodged around him, nearly knocking down an ancient Swahili woman.

Where are we headed? he wondered. *And will there be cake?*

The pain in his side was getting worse. He was starting to lose the grip on his grip. He rounded a corner and stopped. There was nothing ahead but an ancient mosque. His father had vanished.

"This is an inopportune time to get religion."

Bernard turned. His father was standing some thirty yards away, on a decrepit wooden pier. They had run a kilometer in the heat of the day, yet Wendell Franks did not seem the least out of breath. Of course, he could just be putting on a brave face, as Bernard was doing.

"And now that you've got your land legs back—let's go back to sea."

They walked up a short gangplank leading to a fifty-foot steamer that looked like it had been old when Victoria was queen. The engine chugged arrhymically. Alternating balls of black and white smoke belched from the rusty chimney like a College of Cardinals vacillating on the selection of a new Pope.

They were greeted by the filthy German captain, obviously drunk, and his native first mate, obviously devious. As soon as they were aboard, the boat began backing out of the dock. Wendell Franks conferred with the captain and the three of them retired aft where deck chairs had been set up under a dingy gray canopy. The captain, a veteran of the Great War by the name of Bruno Schultz, poured three whiskeys in tin cups. Bernard quickly drained his and gestured for another. Getting hammered, he had discovered on the *Neuralgia,* forestalled his calm-sea sickness. After taking downing a second one, he eased back, took a wide-brimmed white hat out of his grip and fanned himself with it. Noticing a dark smudge on his white pants, he put down his hat, pulled out and unfolded his handkerchief, touched it to his tongue and dabbed at the stain. It smelled worse, but looked no different

"Mussed your pantaloons already, eh?" Wendell Franks said through a thin smile. "Just wait until we get inland."

Bernard shrugged. A side benefit of the seasickness cure was it made his father easier to take.

The ship was lurching toward the mouth of the port, back to the Indian Ocean from which Bernard had arrived not thirty minutes before.

"We seem to be heading in the wrong direction."

Wendell Franks sipped his whiskey, savored it. With his long, hawkish nose and bushy moustache he looked every bit the English major. The old man gazed absentmindedly at an outgoing fishing boat, exhaled and inhaled deeply.

Perhaps he was winded after all, Bernard thought.

"Change in plans, son. It seems the Bosch have gotten a head start. They requisitioned all the lorries and have just now left town."

Spread out behind his father was the panorama of Dar es Salaam, a mélange of German, Asian, English and African architecture as well as, if Bernard's eyes did not deceive him, a Hamburger Heaven.

"The Germans?" Bernard knew from his father's correspondence that they would be heading to the Lushoto region, a few hundred kilometers to the northwest. There, legend said, hidden between the twin peaks of the Usambara Mountains, lived a strange people. This was the first he'd heard about a rival expedition.

"We'd never beat them in a race overland. So we're headed up the coast to Tanga. That should cut our trek by a third."

Captain Schultz, already on his second shot, looked alarmed.

"Tanga? I thought you said Panga?"

"No, you fool! Tanga. Tanga!"

The captain yelled something in Swahili. His first mate yelled something back. The angry exchange continued for several minutes. Knives were brandished in a playful fashion.

Finally, Captain Schultz poured himself a third shot and said, "Tanga it is. But still the same fee, eh?"

Bernard had studied his maps on the voyage and knew that starting from Tanga would shorten their hike. But he also knew they would face tougher terrain and was glad he remembered to pack his gurkhas and calamine lotion.

There was a large boom from the engine room. The shock wave spilled Bernie's drink, which was just as well since he would have preferred something with ice in it. There was a moment of silence as the ship drifted, dead in the water, broken by a single but clear fricative that required no translation. Captain Schultz opened a hatch, releasing a plume of gray smoke and two frenzied crew members. The first mate joined them. There was more yelling and some ill-mannered punching and chest-poking. The captain then shoved the other three back inside and closed the hatch on them.

"No problem. It seems the ship requires a few minor repairs," Captain Schultz said when he had returned to his passengers. "Nothing to worry about. However, we cannot depart until tomorrow morning."

Wendell Franks did a slow burn, and Bernard expected him to blow up. However, he simply drained his drink and glanced fondly at his empty tin cup as if he were enjoying an aged brandy at the club.

"I will help you with the repairs," he said calmly. "I'm quite handy."

"I'll lend any assistance I can as well."

"Nonsense, Bernard. You don't know the first thing about engines."

Bernard tried to correct his father, but it was a useless endeavor. Instead, he agreed to run some errands in town. It would give him a chance to explore the city and, just possibly, track down Gertrude.

He found her, not surprisingly, in a German sausage shop. She had made camp at a table in the shade, drinking coffee and chewing on jerky. As Bernard approached, he noticed that her weak gray eyes were straining to focus on a book of Seleucid poetry.

"Brushing up on your Aramaic?" he asked suavely.

Gertrude looked up, irritated until she recognized the intruder. She flashed a smile with her large, white teeth. Bernard noticed a bit of brown stuff stuck between her upper left canine and incisor. His heart fluttered.

"Mr. Franks!" she cried.

She jumped up and hugged him strenuously. Three vertebrae popped. She stepped back to give him the once over and he did the same. She was the full package all right: five foot ten and broad-shouldered, with a nose that demanded attention. Bernard, suddenly self-conscious, looked down at his clothes. The stains seemed to have multiplied.

One day with my father and already I'm falling apart.

"Research," Gertrude explained after he had joined her at the table.

Bernie laughed. It was wonderful to be young and free and somewhere so exotic with a girl so intelligent. And a girl.

"Research? What are you looking for: the Holy Grail or the Ark of the Covenant?"

Gertrude frowned. "Don't be ridiculous. But yes, perhaps I'll find evidence of Jewish resettlement here. At least that's my theory. And then I will be famous." But she put the book away.

The waiter came. Bernard ordered ginger tea.

"I didn't see you when we disembarked."

"We were—I was in a hurry. But now I am not."

"So you're part of an expedition. You didn't mention it on the ship."

"Sort of." She crossed her legs and hugged herself; not exactly a gesture of openness. "I must go." She rose and dropped a few marks on the table.

Bernard took hold of one of her bony elbows.

"Please. I didn't mean to be nosy. It's just that, well, I have the day to kill and—"

Gertrude sucked her teeth and then smiled. The food particle had disappeared. "I'm going to an apothecary outside of town if you would like to join me."

They spent the day together. The sun was hot but they easily avoided it in various stores and shops. Dar es Salaam was surprisingly metropolitan (although Bernard never did find that Hamburger Heaven). Gertrude said nothing more about her expedition and Bernard was likewise tight-lipped about his father's plans. It was apparent, though, from her self-assured manner that this was not her first trip away from Heidelberg.

While browsing the bazaar Bernard again noticed Gertrude was severely near-sighted. She held each curio close to her face, and no vendor's stall was safe when she was in full stride.

"I have glasses," she admitted, "but I refuse to wear them. Perhaps I am too vain."

After Bernard had dropped off supplies at the boat (his father was below, lecturing the engineer) he met up with Gertrude at a local dive they had spotted earlier in the day. They dined on succulent grubs and rice, washed down with two bottles of German Riesling. Gertrude, with her bad vision, thought she was eating shrimp.

The sun fell quickly over the western mountains as the two walked hand in hand back to the harbor, reluctant to say good-bye. Their mutual affection was further cemented by an exchange of gifts they had purchased during their time together. Bernard gave Gertrude a pocket version of the *Necronomicon* and she surprised him with a shriveled yam that held the soul of a cursed farmer.

Wendell Franks was far from happy about his son's dalliance.

"Women!" he snorted. "You don't see me mucking about with them."

"But you're married. To mother."

"And a fat lot of good came from it," Wendell said, peering pointedly at Bernard.

That night, lying in his hammock on deck, medicated with alcohol and listening to the somnolent mutterings of this father, Bernard thought about Gertrude. Would he see her again? Was she, as he suspected, a part of the competing Nazi expedition? Bernard frowned. He didn't think much of the National Socialists, although he had to admit they had a certain fashion sense.

They departed just after sunrise. The boat sputtered and smoked as before, but the chugging seemed less ominous. The seas were calm for the most part. They made a stop in Zanzibar. Captain Schultz did a regular trade run from Dar es Salaam to the island nation, then up to Panga and back. The drunken captain had misunderstood and thought the Franks expedition was headed for Panga, which was why the crew had balked at the added stop in Tanga.

The team disembarked late in the day: the two Franks and a pair of wise-cracking porters. After a night on the beach, they began their hike. Of the trek through the lowlands Bernard remembered little save the horseflies. It was tough going, even with all of them using machetes, but by the end of the second day the dense foliage gave way to grassland. Bernard, who had suffered calluses, sore muscles and caffeine withdrawal the first two days, was now beginning to enjoy the adventure. The higher they climbed, the less they were bothered by heat and insects. The yelps of the hyenas soothed rather than frightened him at night. And the porters knew many amusing dirty jokes (of which Wendell strongly disapproved).

They were averaging twenty-five to thirty kilometers a day, yet the elder Franks was not satisfied. One night, as they neared Lushoto, Bernard asked his father about the rush.

"Does it matter if the Germans get there before us? I mean, can't we share the discovery—assuming there is anything to be discovered?"

Wendell's sneer looked like a snarl in the light of the campfire. "Apparently you've had your nose buried too deep in your physics books to notice what's going on in Europe. These scientists are funded by a branch of the Nazi Ahnenerbe. On the face of things, they are simply archeologists. But their real mission is to investigate ancient myths in the hope of finding super weapons. In this case, their expedition is looking for a strange race of humans, although how they intend to weaponize them is not clear to me."

Bernard lit a cigarette in the fire. It was a Turkish Dandy, a caustic brand and the only one available in Tanga.

"You mean a superman? An ubermensch?"

"Bah. More like an untermensch. We are searching for the elusive vole people." But he would explain no further, only saying, "You'll see for yourself soon enough."

After ten or twelve days (Bernard lost count) they came within view of the Usambara Mountains. He could see the coffee brown cliff rising through the afternoon rain clouds. They were marked with vertical striations and flanked by the two lofty peaks that looked eerily like a brassiere Janet Leigh would wear. Bernard thought of Gertrude.

The sky was clear and moonless and the shadow of the mountain made the stars all the clearer. They had made camp in the broken rocks at the base of the cliff. The porters, huddled in their wool blankets announced that they would go no farther. "It is a dangerous climb and nothing good lives there," one of them said. Bernard pressed them for more information but they remained silent.

That night, as they sat shivering in the dark (Wendell had insisted they not light a fire so that he could more easily espy any sign of the Nazi expedition), his father explained their true mission.

It seemed that the vole people were not alone on the mountain. For many years they had been under observation by a mad Belgian biologist by the name of Professor Flekeman. Bernard had heard the name in connection with cross-breeding. It was said he had combined the genes of a canine and a roll bug to create a dog that could roll over end on end, garnering interest from both in the scientific and vaudeville communities.

According to Wendell Franks, Flekeman's research had greatly advanced since then. The Nazis were here to recruit the professor at all costs—and Wendell had been sent by the British Military to counter-recruit him.

"You really think there will be another world war?"

"It's only a matter of time," Wendell said, slapping a spider off his knee.

Afterward, Bernard was left to his own thoughts beneath the alien constellations of the Southern Hemisphere. He thought about their immediate mission, of course, but also about his upcoming year of study at Oxford. Would he be up to the challenge? Both were golden opportunities to disappoint his father. Then, unbidden, came a happier thought: Gertrude. He clutched his yam and drifted off to sleep.

Early the next morning the two Franks began their treacherous ascent. The porters, who had agreed to wait indefinitely at the base camp, suggested climbing near what they joking called the Eastern Cup. This would keep the Bernard and Wendell in the sun longer into the afternoon.

It was later that day, as the duo crept carefully up the prominent cleavage of the Usambara, that Bernard first saw the pictograms: a long line, rounded at one end and intersected by two perpendicular scratches. The mark of the vole people.

"I'm sorry. Did you say mole people?" Dr. Driple, who had in fact been half-dozing, sat up at the mention of the word.

"No. vole people. V as in voluminous," Dr. Franks said. But he was thinking back on those pictograms. They reminded him of something else. But what?

The therapist looked at his wristwatch. "What does any of this have to do with your mother?"

STELLA!

Wednesday had been a busy one. Two meetings wedged between two visits to the new Wang's Cajun Deli.

Wang's looked the same from the outside: the oversized eyeglasses, neon shrimp and chop suey messaging. Inside was a different story. For one thing, it was well lit.

"I cleaned the windows," Stella drawled as she refilled a copper's clean white coffee cup (with matching saucer!). "Reckon nobody's done that in thirty years."

Counters and booths, once a uniform dark brown, threw off actual color. Chrome coat racks shone. The floor looked clean enough to eat off of—and so did the plates.

"What is this?" Dr. Franks had sipped his sugar-laden java, found it disconcertingly smooth and aromatic.

"I cleaned the machine, hon."

He didn't like the new Wang's. It was too bright, too good. Emptier, too. Or did the daylight only reveal a perennial lack of clientele?

Stella herself made the doctor uneasy. Not her appearance, of course. She was a big-boned, thirty-something woman with an aggressively friendly manner, shoulder-length hair (without the scarf he could see it was indeed red), big straight teeth and a man's gait—no doubt due to her being from West Virginia coal country.

Indeed, in just his short time at the counter (his corner booth was occupied by plumbers she had hired to resurrect the ladies' room), and in spite of her dashing about, Dr. Franks had learned much about the new owner. And vice versa.

"I had to get out, hon" Stella had told him, leaning over the counter and invading his personal space. "Back there, I'm an aged widower." Her husband had died two years previous in a mining accident and she had used the insurance money to move to the city. When Gus, the old owner, saw the cash, he grabbed it and took off.

By the time the doctor had finished breakfast ("It's on the house, handsome.") Stella was acting like an old friend. Or sister. Or, well, something. "You go get 'em," she said concerning his two meetings. She even made him promise to stop by afterward.

He met Phelpsy at Grand Central Station and they took the subway to Long Island. There, in a swanky hotel by the ocean, they met with the vice president of design from General Motors. Dr. Franks wore his good suit. As an explorer who had been to all eight continents, the doctor was not intimidated by wealth as long as he was sporting his gray wool double-breasted jacket with the brown elbow patches.

The meeting started in promising fashion. Dr. Franks and Phelpsy were led to the vice president's hotel suite. Two GM engineers were also in attendance, and even knew of the doctor by reputation. Phelpsy was clear-eyed and sober, although his pencil moustache reminded Dr. Franks of the bad guy in a Commander Cody serial. Drinks were served.

The invention in play was called the shortwave vehicle lock, a small device that would lock or unlock all the doors of a car from a distance. It was after the doctor had explained and demonstrated the device that things went wrong.

"Where would you keep this gizmo?" one engineer asked.

"It clips to your keys."

"If you have your keys why would you need the gizmo?" the other engineer asked.

"It locks all the doors at once—or unlocks them."

"Isn't Packard coming out with automatic door locks next year?" That was the first engineer.

The doctor was flummoxed. Even the elbow patches weren't helping. Phelpsy jumped in.

"Guys, with this gizmo you can unlock the doors from a distance so you can jump right in without fumbling with your keys."

Then the vice president, who had up until then been focused on cleaning some eggs benedict off his tie, said, "What's that going to save you—like a second?"

Minutes later, Dr. Franks and Phelpsy found themselves out in the hallway. The consensus seemed to be that the shortwave vehicle lock was crazier than the last idea the doctor had pitched them—a giant balloon that would burst open during a crash to protect the driver. (*Try the toy companies*, had been their response to that one.)

Disheartened, the two stopped for sandwiches and got back to Grand Central Station by 1 p.m. From there it was a short walk to the Plaza for their second meeting, with the A&P bigwigs. That one didn't go any better.

"I thought for sure they'd go for your idea," Phelpsy said. He was jotting on his tip sheet while they rode the subway. "It's genius."

The genius invention was a plastic shopping bag. Phelpsy thought they would appreciate the fact that their own bag (the good kind with the twine handles) had inspired the idea. The doctor's plastic version was strong, cheap, lightweight and had holes for handles. Superior in every way to a paper bag. It could even be ground up and made into new bags (something the doctor called *re-usaging*).

The bigwigs had not seen it that way. "We don't think our customers want to carry their groceries home in sacks," one of them had said with a derisive sniff.

Later, Dr. Franks checked the newspapers at Einstein's. A group of jockeys had mysteriously disappeared from Pimlico, but the doctor was steering clear of anything involving short men. Homoscience would have to wait for some other sucker to pioneer it, he thought, reminding himself that pioneers had a high mortality rate. Then Einstein started talking about a performance of a song from *Carousel* on *Lawrence Welk* so the doctor told him to shut up and took a walk.

He found his way to Ace-Descent Laboratory Supply, hoping it would cheer him up. It didn't. They had moved the burnt lab coat he had pointed out on his previous visit, and carefully folded a sleeve over the burn hole. But the source of the problem, the oversized magnifying glass, was still in the window, its focused beam now deforming a bin of plastic tubing.

He didn't want to do anything. He wanted to hide in his basement. Instead, for some reason he couldn't explain—perhaps because he had promised—he returned to Wang's.

It was just after 3 p.m. and Stella was ushering out the last customer. Wang's was not open for dinner.

"Doc! Come on in!" She gestured to the corner. "Your booth is open. Gimme a sec and you can tell me all about it."

Dr. Franks poured himself a cup of coffee and had just stirred in the last of the sugar cubes when she returned. Her apron gone, the skirt of her red checkered gingham dress flounced as she walked.

"Just fixing my face," she announced as she sat down on the same side of the table. "Whoa! You're a big one. Let me fix your collar. There."

Dr. Franks moved as far back against the wall as possible. He looked around nervously, but there was no help and no escape.

There was a quick tug at his throat. Was she straightening his tie? He coughed.

"Aw hon, am I crowding you?" She backed away three centimeters, straightened up and set her hands in her lap like a grade school student. She smelled of violets and bacon. "Okay. So tell Stella how it went."

He told her.

"Doc," she said when he was through. "We dreamers gotta stick together. You're having some tough times. You ever need a friendly ear or a good cup of joe, I'll be right here." She shouldered him affectionately into the wall.

The doctor frowned. "Sure. Thanks. Sure."

Stella laughed; a boisterous guffaw.

"I mean it now. Any time." She stood up. "Now go home and invent something. I got work to do."

So he tinkered in his basement, but his heart wasn't in it. The bowl outside the window was empty, but whether that was due to Dash or birds or the bluster of November winds he didn't know. His mind was on other things. Failure. Stella. Money. And his father.

Perhaps, and his heart dropped at the thought, it was time to give it all up and get a real job.

THE VOLE PEOPLE

"You were talking about your mother."

It was the second session. The two doctors had taken their places, Driple in his wingback chair and Franks on the leather couch. The former kept glancing at his wristwatch, as if to emphasize that he was conducting the sessions gratis.

"We were discussing my father. Major Wendell Franks."

"Ah yes." Dr. Driple leaned toward and steepled his fingers, then thought better of it and pulled back. "The molemen."

"The vole people." Dr. Franks settled in.

"Not long after finding the peculiar pictograph—" He paused, remembering the odd marking. "Um, we reached an opening in the cliff. Only four feet high but obviously manmade. And given the draft that was blowing through it, not a dead end. We crawled inside, my father leading the way..."

The tunnel was pitch black, and the only sounds were the scuffling and complaining of his father. Somehow, one of Bernard's garters had disappeared and his left sock was drooping. The floor, alternating between rock and hard dirt, led gently yet steadily upward. The draft had ceased, possibly because Wendell was blocking the passage. Bernard, prone to claustrophobia, opted to focus on the first unrelated thought that came to him. Unfortunately, it was his relationship with his father. Try as he might, he just could not please the man. Or maybe– He stopped crawling. Maybe he was being too hard on the old fellow.

"Father," he whispered.

No answer.

"Father, just tell me once and for all: Are you proud of me?"

Silence.

I should have known better; he's probably composing the perfect insult in his head, Bernard thought. But when more time passed and the silence held, Bernard realized to his horror that his father was no longer ahead of him.

He whispered his father's name a few times, but the only reply was an echo. Shouting seemed like a bad idea; he didn't know who or what else might be in the tunnels. Were they not here to look for a strange race of people? Suppressing his fear he crawled forward as quickly as he could and banged his head against a hard dirt object.

The silence remained, only now joined by a throbbing pain. He touched his forehead. No blood. He felt around in front of him and discerned two facts: the wall here was dirt and not stone–which was why he hadn't cracked his skull open–and the tunnel forked off in two directions.

But which one had his father taken?

He risked striking a match. There was no trace of his father, nor any indication of which direction he had gone. The left opening led down, the right up. As the match burned down he considered his options. Going down led further into the mountains, but going up would be harder.

He chose the right tunnel; his father always chose the hard road.

"I'm sorry—is this going to take much longer? I have an electro-shock therapy at 3:30."

"I'm condensing things as it is," Dr. Franks grumbled.

"As long as we're leading to something," Dr. Driple said, trying not to look at his watch.

Dr. Franks settled back into the upholstery.

"I took the right tunnel, the one going up. Soon I thought I could see the tunnel walls, and not long after that I was sure. After another thirty yards I emerged onto what must have been a plateau between the two peaks. But instead of grassland I was in a small clearing surrounded by towering conifers. My father was nowhere in sight.

"Throwing caution to the wind I called out. After a minute or so I heard the crunching of dry pine needles—someone or some thing was approaching.

"It was not my father. Instead, several odd creatures emerged from the forest. They were something like pygmies, but unlike any I had encountered before. The figures shared many of the features of central Africans yet were pale in color. Their noses were long and delicate, and they wriggled them often, like rabbits. It was hard to determine their average height because they tended to crawl on all fours. I knew then that I had found that strange and mysterious race—the vole people.

"They were skittish. Yet after several moments of hesitation and gesticulating amongst themselves, they suddenly charged me. Before I could react I was being carried with surprising quickness through the forest.

"I was so shocked I didn't even resist. The firs were amazingly tall—perhaps one hundred feet—and I wondered who had planted them and when and what would happen if you dropped a penny from the top. But I knew you couldn't have voles (or, apparently, vole people) without conifers; the needles are an essential part of their diet.

"After about half an hour we came to a large clearing. A crude lean-to was situated almost dead center. There was a fire and, under the lean-to, a big-nosed, statuesque young woman. Gertrude!

"Despite our desperate situation, the reunion was a happy one. The vole people, far from being a danger, seemed happy that we knew each other. They soon went about their business, which consisted of foraging for food and jumping in fright every time they heard a twig snap.

"It seemed Gertrude had traveled with the very same Nazi expedition my father had been concerned about. It was being led by her uncle, a Colonel Erwin von Kapukt. However, unlike my father and the mysterious Professor Flekeman, Gertrude was on her own archeological quest—searching for the legendary Ark of the Covenant. She had left the Nazi expedition two days earlier—the day they arrived at the mountain—to conduct her own search.

"After having a good laugh at her expense (*Ark of the Covenant—that's a good one!*) I explained my situation. She thought there was a good chance that my father, having taken a downward tunnel, was now an unwilling guest of Professor Flekeman ("He's a strong-willed man, a brilliant man; surprisingly considerate," she had noted) in the massive cavern that served as his laboratory. However, it was equally as likely that he had come to a dead end. Over countless generations, the vole people had dug a literal maze of tunnels. Gertrude thought she could lead me back to the main tunnel, from which she had emerged. So, after a quick meal of landjaeger and Sixlets, we set off. It was early afternoon, with plenty of daylight left. But as night fell we found ourselves back at the clearing. Gertrude, despite her book smarts, had a bad sense of direction.

"As the days went on, we fell into something of a routine. In the mornings I would search for an entrance to Flekeman's cavern, where, I hoped, I would find my father. The vole people were a mixed blessing in this regard: they would lead me to, and often into, tunnel entrances, but most led to their nurseries or stashes of fir needles.

"Afternoons we spent looking for the Lost Ark. Personally, I thought she was crazy looking for it there as the smart money put it in Zimbabwe. But I was in love. I spent hours walking behind her, marveling at the graceful way she swatted a horsefly or hacked the branch off an offending acacia tree. She was a determined woman with a strong desire for success.

"At night we would sit downwind of the fire so the smoke would ward off the gnats. She would recite Schopenhauer and I would play ragtime tunes with a comb and tissue. We rationed our meals, not wishing to impose on the vole people. Not that they weren't willing to share, but their staple was an unappetizing dish called *ukul*, made from fir needles, crushed centipede and yam paste. They would pat the mixture into balls and, after letting them dry for several days, store the balls in sacks tied around their waists. Ukul balls were not only nourishing but hard and aerodynamic, making them ideal for fending off amorous civet.

"One afternoon, while rounding the Eastern Cup, we came upon the ruins of a lost city. Based on the state of decay of the towering parapets, Gertrude estimated the place to have been unoccupied for several centuries whereas I, judging by the empty Pepsi bottles, argued for a more recent date. Nevertheless, we ran across several items that linked the site to the Great Zimbabwe Civilization of the Fourteenth Century. Our vole-ish companions showed no special regard for the place, but when you're basically a giant mouse you tend not to get excited about architecture.

"Gertrude disappeared into a doorway. Moments later, she was crying for my help. I ran to her aid, thinking she was in trouble, and instead found her caressing a large metal tub. It was perhaps a meter and a half long and half as wide, with an opening on the top flanked by two wing-like appendages.

"'We've got to take it back to camp,' she said, her gray eyes squinting with excitement.

"When I asked how we would lift it, she pointed out the four metal rings, one at each corner. We trimmed down two sturdy branches and slid them through. The tub or urn or whatever it was was heavy but not unmanageable. I also found an old generator, probably from a failed expedition (which explained the Pepsi bottles), and persuaded Gertrude to take it back with us as well.

"We did not speak as we made our way. But I wondered, Had she really found the Ark of the Covenant? And if she had, how stupid did that make me look for not even being able to find my own father?

"That night, as we slept under the stars, breathing in the acrid smoke from the fire, I made it to second base but got thrown out trying for a triple.

"'I'm saving myself for marriage,' Gertrude explained while bending my thumb backwards. 'The man I marry must be a great man. Will you be a great man, Bernard?'

"I promised her I would. But it didn't get me any further that night.

"We were now joined in one thing, however. We now had a common purpose. For, having found what she hoped was the Ark Gertrude was as anxious as me to find Flekeman's cavern and, thereby, her uncle, Colonel von Kapukt. We had a short-wave radio, but the battery was weak. I reasoned that if we could fix the old generator we had found we could perhaps send an S.O.S. All it needed was a way to crank it. It was Gertrude who had the solution—a way to generate all the power we would need.

"After a week of chopping and tinkering we had constructed an eight-foot-high wheel suspended on an axle.

Running on the wheel cranked the generator. The wheel wasn't for us, but the vole people, who, as Gertrude had hoped, took to it like, well, rodents."

Dr. Driple coughed politely and eyed his watch. Dr. Franks took the hint.

"We made radio contact the very next morning. I should say Gertrude did. Her uncle, Colonel von Kapukt, was relieved to hear from her and said they would be out the next day to retrieve us both. It wasn't a moment too soon as we had run out of food and were on the verge of trying the ukul balls.

"The next morning, to pass the time, we re-examined the Ark. It had similarities to the biblical version: gold inlay, rings for carrying and two opposing figures on the top that could be interpreted as angels. But there were oddities as well. Specifically, the flanged opening in the lid, a feature never mentioned in the Pentateuch. Gertrude posited several ingenious purposes for this opening, but at last and too gleefully I pointed out its obvious function. In truth, this ark was nothing more than a portable royal outhouse, and the "angels" merely decorative handles for the convenience of the user.

"'At least now we have a first-class bed pan,' I told her. Her response was to pry loose the flanged seat and hit me in the cranium. I've been tolerant of people's religious beliefs ever since.

"Our animated discussion was cut short by the arrival of the Nazis. Half a dozen soldiers, plus a motorcycle. Colonel von Kapukt, a serious young man who looked to suffer from chronic indigestion, was in the sidecar. The vole people, who knew a bad thing when they saw it, ran for the forest.

"Gertrude's reunion with her uncle was far from warm. In fact, he ordered the soldiers to bind our arms. Gertrude was indignant. I shrugged. I mean, they *were* Nazis. My sole regret was not being able to say good-bye to our vole-ish hosts. But they'd always have the wheel to remember us by.

"We were led to a massive, sloping cave opening some twenty meters wide and ten feet high, not more than a kilometer from the clearing. The fact that we didn't discover it earlier says much about my bad luck and Gertrude's nearsightedness. The tunnel led into the ground. In a few minutes we found ourselves in a huge rectangular cavern cut into the rock and lit by electric torches. At the far end, on a raised wooden platform, were two men in safari attire. One of them was my father.

"'Here's my son Bernard,'" he said without fanfare. 'What took you so long?'

"'I went up. It was the hard road,' I told him.

"'You coward. You know I always go down. Down to danger.'

"The other man, a tall blonde albino, was the infamous Professor Bruno Flekeman of Belgium.

"Flekeman, as mentioned before, was studying the vole people, who through a unique combination of adaptation, inbreeding and unmentionable practices had inherited the traits of the tiny mouse-like creatures.

"The soldiers untied us. There was nowhere we could go, after all. My father, it seemed, had only just been discovered himself. Soon after we parted ways he had become lost in the tunnels, surviving on lichen and ground water until coming upon Flekeman's underground compound. After that, he remained hidden, stealing food when necessary and spying whenever possible. He had been captured only a few days before our arrival.

"The professor was more than happy to show us his operation. He had converted this large natural cave into a research lab, where he conducted tests on the vole people. The tests were horrific: multiple choice, true/false and the dreaded essay question. Even pop quizzes. Many gave up on life, while others had to repeat the semester.

"The Nazis had made Flekeman an irresistible offer: In exchange for unlimited funding and a full benefits package Flekeman would create an *unter*-race of mindless fighting men with the intelligence of a human (or at least a Bavarian) and the abilities of an animal. Apparently, the only variable left undetermined was the specific animal.

"'Think of a man with the strength of an elephant,' Flekeman postulated. 'The thick hide of an elephant, the proboscis of an elephant, the memory of an elephant. Well, obviously I'm leaning toward elephant.'

"For an evil scientist, Flekeman displayed a strong need for approval. During the tour he would often stop and say, 'That's not horribly evil, is it? I mean, if I don't exploit these vole people someone else will. Probably someone a lot more evil than me. Like that Mengele fellow.' Then he'd offer us some biscuits.

"My father was no help in persuading Flekeman to side with the Allies. In his typically off-putting way, he criticized everything about the man, from his methodology to his wardrobe. There was also Colonel von Kapukt, who was not one to take no for an answer.

"All this was a sad turn of events for the vole people, for, as horrible as the tests had been, their chances of continued survival once word of their docile nature got out would be worse. One could only hope that the population would eventually evolve into full humanity or devolve back to vole-hood. Either way they'd be a lot less creepy to look at.

"However, my father and I had more immediate concerns.

"'I'm sorry to be such a rude host,' Flekeman told us without a hint of irony, 'but there's a U-boat waiting for me in Zanzibar. I'm going to be a Nazi scientist!'

"'What about us?' I asked, though I didn't look forward to hearing the answer.

"'I'm afraid I'm going to have to eliminate you, Franks,' he said. 'That's not too evil of me, is it? I mean, if I don't these

Nazis will, and they'll make an awful mess of it. I'm doing you a favor, really.'

"'Uncle, is this true?' Gertrude demanded of Colonel von Kapukt.

"'I'm afraid so,' the colonel admitted. 'My soldiers can't hit the broad side of a zeppelin. An execution wouldn't be fun to watch.'"

Dr. Driple coughed loudly and tapped his wristwatch.

"It wasn't long before the two of us were tied up and led to a large tunnel that sloped downward into darkness. We were told the other end opened on the cliff face.

"'Wish me luck,' Flekeman said. Then he slapped his forehead. 'Sorry—that was really inappropriate.'

"At this point, one of the Germans cut our bonds. They had lined the floor of the tunnel with pine needles so that with one push we would slide down, be spit out of the cliff face and plummet to the broken rocks far below. It would look like a climbing accident."

"Was there something in all this about your father?" Dr. Driple interrupted.

"Getting there!" Dr. Franks said. "The Nazis pushed us down the slope. With their guns trained on us we had no choice but to let them. Gertrude ran up to me, but words failed her. Finally, she took my hand and said, 'I think you're cute,' Hand to God, she said that. Just like that. Then she gave me a long, lingering handshake before I was pulled away. My last sight as they pushed us down the slope was of Professor Flekeman putting a comforting arm around her.

"I flailed my arms wildly, hoping to find a handhold. Finally my left hand gripped something—my father's wrist! There was light up ahead, which meant we were approaching the cliff. I dug my heels in and, despite my father's additional weight, was able to stop my progress less than a yard before the opening and the precipitous drop. My father was hanging over the edge.

"'Quit showing off!' he told me."

"What a horrible experience for you." Dr. Driple was putting on his overcoat.

"Then my father began to slip," Franks continued. "I tried to pull him up, but it was all I could do hold him. He looked up at me and whispered, 'You call that a grip?' Then he fell. His last words as he plummeted to the ground:

"'You've always been...

"...a major disappoint...

"...to me.'"

Dr. Driple had the doorknob in one hand and was rattling his keys with the other. Dr. Franks recognized it as classic leave-taking behavior.

"Boy, that's really, really sad. Have you thought of getting counseling?"

FRITTERS

Thursday. Of the worst week in Dr. Franks' memory. Except that it wasn't, because now he vividly remembered that tragic week seventeen years before when he had lost his father and the young woman he might have loved. Of course it could be argued that the reliving of those painful events, combined with experiencing those of the current week, did indeed make the current week the worst one in his memory. Either way it was no picnic.

"Mother, am I a failure?"

Dr. Franks addressed the question to the door of the Kelvinator, which hid most of Mrs. Franks.

"What the hell kind of stupid question is that?" She asked, followed immediately by, "Can pickles go bad?"

Dr. Franks groaned. It was hard to talk to her when she was cleaning the refrigerator. Now, for instance, she was tossing questionable items into the metal trash can she had dragged over for the purpose. In her day she had been quite a tough bird, in turns a mechanic, radical nun and aviatrix. Her marriage to Wendell Franks had been both unorthodox and inconvenient. But since her husband's death she had focused on providing as normal a life as possible for Bernard. Given her history, this consisted mostly of heating up TV dinners and keeping her salty language in check.

The room smelled of sour milk.

"It's just that—I was thinking about dad. You know."

Mrs. Franks continued to clean as she talked.

"Let me tell you something about Wendell. *(Thud.)* The first time I met him he had the nerve to tell me that women shouldn't have the vote. *(Crash.)* Can you imagine that? *(Clank.)* And me a suffragette! *(Boom. Swoosh.)* I smacked him right on top of his pointy head. *(Clunk.)* Your father was a great man and we loved each other in our own way. *(Plop.)* But that moron never learned to think before opening his big British trap."

"So he didn't think I was a failure?"

"Son, he thought everybody was a failure. She paused. "Did you bring home an order of noodles and gray fuzz? *(Thud.)* Anyway, the point is you are definitely not a failure. I've always thought you were a success for following your own road in life. You're a brilliant inventor—and that homo thing sounds good too. Whatever you do, I'll be proud of you." After a short silence, she poked her head around the door, her shrewd eyes peering in his general direction. "Bernie, if I push too hard to get you to move out it's only because I want you to have a life for yourself. *(Shatter.)* Not be stuck here with me."

Dr. Franks was actually choked with emotion. His mother never talked to him like this, possibly because he had never given her the chance. Twice he started to say something, but the words caught on the lump in his throat.

"Thank you, mother," he croaked finally. "That really means a lot."

Mrs. Franks stopped rooting around. Now, standing at her full height, the top of her round gray head was visible.

"Come here, Bernie. Your momma needs you."

"Yes, mother!"

She held out a ceramic container.

"Taste this pot roast and tell me if it's gone bad."

That morning at Wang's, Dr. Franks slumped in his corner booth under the poorly-rendered mural of the Grand Canal, picking at pineapple fritters and cured ham with an escargot fork left over from the establishment's days as a French bistro. His mac, fresh from a thorough scrubbing by Mrs. Franks, looked older and paler than before. As did the man. Unshaven cheeks combined with the wildness of the existing chin beard to create a goat-like visage.

"Anything good in the paper, hon?" Stella asked.

Dr. Franks turned the *Times* face down.

"I'm perusing the want ads," he announced with a bravado that fooled neither of them. "It's time to get a real job."

Stella sat down next to him and examined the pad of paper he had been scribbling on. The beginnings of a résumé.

"What kind of position are you looking for?"

"Rocket scientist. Or secretarial."

Stella gave him a solemn nod.

"I'm having trouble thinking of a third reference," he said, brightening a little. Problem-solving always cheered him up. "Right now I've got von Braun and Linus Pauling."

"What about Heisenberg?"

"He's a bit uncertain."

The door bells chimed. Stella rose.

"Well, I'd hire you here if you had any cooking skills."

"Really?"

"Sure. I gotta be ready when business picks up. Can you fry an egg?"

Dr. Franks thought for a moment.

"Theoretically."

But Stella had already marched off to greet the new customer. Dr. Franks watched her, amazed again at her solidity and balance. He reckoned it would take at least three men to knock her down. Yep, Stella was a good egg. She encouraged him to dress better and bathe regularly, but not in a mean way—and even though she barely knew him had offered to lend Dr. Franks money (he had turned her down). She wasn't the bosomy blonde he was typically attracted to—but then the bosomy blondes never seemed to reciprocate.

His thoughts were interrupted by a horse laugh; Stella was feigning amusement at the newcomer's joke. He older man was one of only two others in the diner. Dr. Franks turned the Times back to the front page and a story of the disappearance of several sewer workers. Had he been in a more positive state he would have inventoried all the recent disappearances—the jockeys, the sanitation men—as homoscientific clues in the Midget Murder Spree case. But he didn't want to relive that failure. Not just yet. He put the writing tablet and newspaper into his A&P bag and stood up with a groan. Then he noticed with surprise the food left on his plate.

"Have I been eating fritters!?" he asked no one in particular.

He went to the library to check want ads and see what Clarice the circulation girl was wearing. To his surprise, she was much friendlier—though more conservatively dressed.

"Oh—am I glad to see you." Crystal said, her expression quickly changing from anger to relief. "You wouldn't believe the perverts that have been in here today, all making a beeline for yours truly."

Dr. Franks handed her the request form and noticed with no little sadness the bulky gray wool sweater that covered Caroline from neck to knee.

"Perverts, you say?"

"Yeah. All nerdy little guys, too. It's like the shrimp fleet's in town, if you know what I mean. *Journal of Pseudo-scientific Research?* You're, like, the only one who asks for this one." She turned to get the periodical.

"Little nerdy guys," Dr. Franks mused. "And creepy."

"I'll say. Trying to strike up conversations with me and the whole time looking me up and down. Kind of like you do, except a lot creepier."

Dr. Franks smiled. It was the nicest thing Kitty had ever said to him.

After a moment, Charlene returned.

"Here you go. Funny, but that issue was right in the return bin. Guess someone else reads it after all. Must have been when I was on break. Do you want your *Redbook?*"

Dr. Franks shook his head sadly. It wouldn't be the same with the heavy wool sweater. He turned to go, but stopped. He had to ask.

"Did any of these men try to pick up something heavy?"

Christine frowned. "Are you calling me fat?"

Sitting in his usual spot, he flipped through the new *JPSR*. Not much of interest: Russian scientists claiming they had captured another Yeti, a theory that Jesus was an alien with an aversion to shaving, an exposé on the Girls Scouts.

Dr. Franks stretched, cracked his neck. The room was rather full for a Thursday, the middle tables were filled with short men, uniformly dressed in oversized gray flannel blazers. The doctor noticed a few of the titles they were reading: *Emily Post's Guide to Etiquette, The Power of Positive Thinking,* Horatio Alger stories. *Shrimp fleet indeed,* he thought.

He looked back down at the JPSR. There were pages missing. Perplexed, he flipped back and forth and, sure enough, it went from 18 to 23. According to the table of contents, the missing pages were an essay by a Professor Flekeman of Belgium.

Flekeman? *The* Professor Flekeman? His father's arch enemy Flekeman? It was too much of a coincidence.

Then—crazily, phantasmagorically—he saw the man himself.

Yes. Professor Flekeman was in the middle of the room. Dr. Franks would recognize him anywhere: the thin face with the high cheekbones and eyes sunk deep into the sockets. The apologetic half-smile. And, really, how many albinos did one run across?

He was sitting right in the middle of the shrimp fleet. No—he wasn't sitting. Flekeman was standing, only now he was a mere four feet tall, leaning on a metal cane that looked like a piece of industrial equipment. On further inspection, it looked like a metal leg, complete with black socks and oxfords; it was difficult to say because the short albino was draped in a wide brown cape.

Not wanting to be caught staring, Dr. Franks looked back to his periodical. A sliver of one of the missing folios caught his eye. Half of a circular symbol was visible, inside the circle (or semicircle in this case) was a line with a dot on one end, intersected by three shorter lines.

The same symbol that was on the Societas Homoformicidae cards found on the supposed accident victims. And both similar to the symbol he had seen etched on those mountain cliffs long ago—the symbol of the vole people.

But what did it mean?

No! He was done with that case!

He found himself gazing again at the children's encyclopedia in front of him *(Vol. 12, Phrenology to Psychological Torture)*. Then it hit him. Just as the line crossed by two lines was the symbol of a four-legged creature (the vole), the line crossed by three lines represented a six-legged creature—the ant!

A noise made him look up. He could have sworn he heard another quick shuffling of chairs, like students at the end of a study hall. Flekeman was eyeing him, as were most of his tiny gray flannel followers. Had he been talking out loud? Perhaps he belched in public again? He sniffed. No gassy residue. And Clarisse (Carrie?) hadn't looked up from her filing. Casually, he checked his fly. No, everything was in order.

Carefully, the doctor took out a small black case containing a small pair of scissors and other equipment, snipped off the remaining sliver of one of the missing pages and slipped it into a test tube. This task done, he packed his books, papers and other materials into his A&P shopping bag and dropped off the magazine with Candy(?), who grunted a good-bye without bothering to look up from her *Highlights* magazine. He gave the reference section a quick once-over. The little men were standing at attention, eyes on Flekeman like trained seals.

Dr. Franks headed for the exit.

Behind him he could hear several pairs of footsteps and, louder still, a *pat-pat-click* on the tile floor. He picked up the pace, but the horrible *pat-pat-click* only got closer. An irrational fear overtook him. He dared not look back.

Once outside, he crossed the street and headed east. The foot traffic was lighter than expected so there was no chance of losing himself in a crowd. After two blocks he stopped and pretended to look at an Erector Set in the window of a toy store.

Was he crazy, or could he still hear that *pat-pat-click?* Just when he had convinced himself it was an aural hallucination he caught a sight in the window that made his heart stop. Or rather, in the window's reflection.

Across the street was Flekeman and his little gray men. Dr. Franks recovered himself and hurried away. There was no doubt about it: he was being chased by a man with a cane.

And the man was gaining on him.

PROFESSOR FLEKEMAN

Dr. Franks doubled back toward the library. After a block or so, he looked across the street. There were no signs of his pursuers. Relieved, he slowed his pace. It had been seventeen years, after all; Flekeman may not even have recognized him. Probably, he was overreacting due to the trauma of the prior week, a condition for which he had coined the term *after-the-fact stress response*. The whole thing was silly, really. Probably, it wasn't even Flekeman, and those other men simply librarians from Iowa or some such place at a convention and taking the opportunity to see the Main Library. He took a calming breath, lit a Turkish Dandy and inhaled the acrid, yet soothing smoke.

Then behind him, first as a whisper of a whisper and soon clearly above the soft din of the mid-afternoon foot traffic, was the tell-tale *pat-pat-click*. Dr. Franks glanced quickly over his shoulder and his cigarette dropped to the pavement. Not twenty yards back, he spied the horrible albino cripple.

Hurrying away, the doctor felt a pang of shame. After all, this was the man who killed his father–should he not turn and face him? On the other hand, those little men looked dangerous. He decided it was best to be on the safe side.

He rounded a corner, knowing he would find Einstein's newsstand. Such was the doctor's fear that he was actually glad to see Einstein inside it.

"Shut up, Einstein," the doctor said before adding, "Let me in."

The inane smile never left Einstein's face. He opened the side door and the doctor slipped inside. There was just room enough for him to crouch behind a stack of bundled returns.

"If anybody asks you haven't seen me," Dr. Franks whispered.

The doctor soon heard a man inquiring of Einstein as to location of a "large man unkempt man with crazy eyes and a shopping bag with twine handles." Einstein, standing at the window at the other end of the shack, was playing dumb (not a stretch by any means).

"He would be a doctor," the man said.

Dr. Franks knew the accent. Not German or French. Belgian.

"Let me tell you about doctors," Einstein said. "I went to the hospital because I twisted my ankle and they wanted to do X-rays. I ask them how much that will cost and they say thirty bucks. 'Thirty bucks?' I say. 'What will the X-rays do?' 'Tell us if your ankle is broken,' they say. And I say 'I already know it's broken because it don't work right.' I mean is that crazy or what? Hey, do you like the Lennon Sisters?"

There was a long pause. "If you see the doctor, tell him this: do not make a mountain out of a mole hill—or should I say *vole* hill."

After about ten seconds Einstein said, "Huh. Didn't even buy nothing."

Dr. Franks rose unsteadily, pushing aside the dusty stack of *New York Posts*. Einstein's newsstand had a musty, musky smell that reminded him of that weekend Dash got trapped in the basement. He looked at the finger where the squirrel bit him. It was red. And was he imagining things or did he suddenly crave a glass of water?

"Hey, that was pretty mysterious, huh? I mean that guy was cree-py. You working on another case, doc? Good for you."

"No!" Dr. Franks knew he had said it too loudly. His mouth felt like a cotton ball in the desert. He stepped outside and stood, frowning.

"You need help, doc? A little surveillance? You know me—cool as toast. Hey—you need a gun? My uncle can get you a gun, no problem."

Dr. Franks was about to cut Einstein short with a string of invective. Einstein would talk your ear off if you let him. Still, he did need something.

"You wouldn't happen to have a copy of the latest *Journal of Pseudo-Scientific Research* I could borrow?"

"The *JPSR*? Sure, I got the new issue right here. Good article on flying cars."

Dr. Franks dropped the periodical into his bag. "I shall return it on Monday."

He finished reading the Flekeman article, the one that had been missing from the library. The Belgian was apparently in New York, working on what he called his Manhattan Project. Few specifics were provided about the nature of the work, but Flekeman boasted that it would "change the world."

It was 3 p.m. at Wang's. Dr. Franks, sitting at the counter, took another sip of his disturbingly delicious coffee. The only sounds were the television and Uncle Tonoose banging pots and pans somewhere in the kitchen. An elderly couple camped out in a booth, nursing their tea. Stella was counting her receipts for the day, a pencil behind her ear and a revolver next to the register.

Dr. Franks was trying to make sense of it all. According to the article, Flekeman's work for the Germans had involved trying to infuse arachnid attributes into homo sapiens. It was rumored that by the end of the war he had created a group of spider-men who could climb walls and spin webs out of an unnamed orifice. Now, according to the article, Flekeman had moved on to insects. This was disturbing even to a scientist like Dr. Franks, who had once tried to give a donkey perfect pitch.

He wondered again whatever had become of the vole people. They were not a bad bunch, really. They had even rescued him after his fall (too late for Wendell) and handed him over to the porters waiting at the base of the mountains. (A large deposit of guano had broken his fall and he sustained only minor injuries.) Flekeman had no doubt abandoned the little people, with apologies, to the Nazis.

The article included a photograph. It was Flekeman, standing next to a bunker. The symbol on the door was similar to both that of the Societas Homoformicidae and the vole people—only with four intersecting lines instead of three or two. No doubt, Flekeman had revised the vole people's pictogram to give it eight legs (a spider), and now three lines (six legs) for...

So there was something to the ant theory after all. And Professor Flekeman was behind it. But what was he up to? Did this Manhattan Project have anything to do with the deaths and missing persons cases?

Flekeman was involved somehow—otherwise the man wouldn't have tried to scare him off at the library. Those gray-suited men were part of Flekeman's project. And whatever the project was, it probably wasn't for the good of mankind.

He looked up at the TV. Some panel game show.

Stella turned randomly toward him while doing math in her head, gave him a peculiar smile. It made him uneasy, that smile. The only time Dr. Franks saw that look was when women were pretending to like him in order to get something from him. That was the confusing part—Stella was the one with the money, assuming Wang's didn't go belly up. So why did she look at him like that? Amusement?

"Say doc, why don't we go to a movie tonight, the two of us? It'd get your mind off your troubles. *War of the Worlds* is playing. I hear you find science fiction movies funny."

"Stella, an alien invasion is no laughing matter. They won't be Martians, surely, but—"

"Howdy, friends. It's Dinky Dave, the little man with big deals on Fords!"

"Oh, for—"

"What's the matter, doc?"

"Here's a sweet convertible." The TV showed Dinky Dave standing in front of a slanted, rotating ragtop, with Henna in the passenger seat. *"Sorry fellas—the Lovely Henna is not available."*

"I'd like to see that emergency brake slip and crush him," Dr. Franks said. "That would be good television."

The elderly couple looked up, alarmed.

"Easy, doc. Isn't that the guy who got the restraining order against you?"

"Where'd you hear that?"

"Einstein."

"Einstein needs to shut up."

The television now showed a close-up of Dinky Dave's chubby hand caressing a chrome hood ornament. He was wearing a large pinky ring. And the design on the ring—it couldn't be!—a vertical line with dot on one end, intersected by three shorter lines. Dr. Franks spit his coffee.

"...an amazing offer, citizens. With every purchase this month you gentlemen get an absolutely free membership in the Mighty Antman Club. What is that, you ask? Why, haven't you been watching my commercials? It's only the most amazing self-improvement technique ever. The Mighty Antman Club harnesses the power of the insect kingdom to make any man—no matter how puny—bigger, stronger and more confident. And citizens, I'm not just the owner and founder of the club," he paused to look at Henna, *"I'm a satisfied member."*

"What?" Stella came over, wiped up the coffee. "Too bitter?"

Jung would call it synchronicity. Dr. Franks called it homoscience. Probably, it was dumb luck. Whatever it was, it was too much to ignore.

"Perhaps another time," Dr. Franks said. "I believe I'm back on the case."

BACK ON THE CASE

Still unable to flag a cab, Dr. Franks walked the length of Staten Island to get to the 14th Precinct. His timing couldn't have been better, though—most of the homicide detectives had left for the weekend and Sergeant Dingle would be in the hospital for another week. Inspector Grimes was in a good, or at least passive, mood when the doctor carefully approached his office door. His desktop was clear of tossable objects and he looked to be getting ready to leave himself.

"Doc! Here to make more false accusations?"

Dr. Franks nodded amicably. He had that coming.

"I was hoping to pick up my check."

The inspector took a ledger book from his top drawer.

"I was wondering when you'd come snooping around for that. What did we say—ten bucks a day?"

"Thirteen." Grimes picked up a pen. "I believe I have one day still unpaid."

Grimes cut the check. Dr. Franks thought of mentioning something, and then thought better of it. Better to wait until he had the money.

"Anything else?" he asked, handing over the payment. There was just a trace of suspicion in his tone.

"Now that you mention it." Dr. Franks put the check in his deepest inside pocket, "I had a thought about the case."

"Oh you did?"

"I don't know if you'd have a few minutes."

"Of course." Grimes leaned back and threw his arms up expansively. "It's my fifteenth wedding anniversary. I'm taking the wife out to celebrate. But I always have time for you, doc."

Dr. Franks sat down, cautiously.

"I think this case may be bigger than we had first thought."

"Now, what case would that be?"

"The antmen case."

"The antmen? Oh. You mean the Midget Murder Spree? That case?"

Dr. Franks bit the inside of his cheek. He felt obligated to tell Grimes his suspicions despite the chance of ridicule. Or bruising.

"I would like to report the evidence and my theories, all based on the latest in homoscientific methodology."

The inspector listened without interruption. The doctor talked for seven minutes.

"So," Grimes said when Dr. Franks had finished, "you think a mysterious Nazi–"

"Former Nazi."

"Former Nazi scientist who was six feet tall when he killed your father in the East Indies–"

"East Africa."

"East Africa, is now four feet tall, in New York, and abducting short men in order to create a race of super spider-men–"

"Antmen."

"Your evidence for this consists of an article in a UFO magazine, an overheard remark by an albino and a design on a business card and a pinky ring–"

"And in the UFO magazine."

157

"And based on this you want me to harass Dinky Dave, who just happens to be the one man in the city you hate so much that a judge had to order to stay at least one hundred feet away from him at all times."

"One hundred yards."

Grimes looked at the doctor with one bloodshot eye. "You are so lucky I've been drinking. Get the hell out of here before I dig out my coffee mug."

Back on the street, the doctor almost got a cab. He had the back door open before the driver recognized him and sped off. At least he had been paid, he thought as he patted his chest. The check inside his mac buckled reassuringly. It was too late to cash it so it headed for home.

The meeting with Inspector Grimes had gone as expected. Which was why he had stopped in the evidence room first. He didn't take anything–that would be wrong. He simply wrote down the phone numbers of the dead men's next of kin.

Once back home he called each of them, telling them he was a Sergeant Dingle so they wouldn't hang up. Sure enough, all of them–the editor, the choir director, the accountant and the vaudevillian–had all purchased cars from Dinky Dave Ford in the past six months. Curious.

He looked out the basement window. The tree was bare. Dash was nowhere in sight.

What did this new piece of evidence tell him? Not much.

Like it or not, he'd have to go see Dinky Dave.

Tavern on the Green, for those not intimately familiar with New York City, is a fancy bistro in the heart of the city. In the summer, one can dine al fresco on a large patio overlooking a pitch and putt in Central Park (hence the name). The rich, famous and infamous are often seen there. It was well known that Dinky Dave had a corner booth reserved for Friday nights.

And no sooner had the aforementioned Dinky Dave settled in than he was approached by the most unkempt of waiters. A large man with a wild beard and wilder hair. His tuxedo was several sizes too small. Worse still, there was something horribly familiar about the look in the large man's googily eyes.

"You!" Dinky Dave cried.

Nearby diners stopped mid-bite. Adlai Stevenson, sitting at a nearby table with Jack Parr and Bennett Cerf, rolled his eyes before returning to a dry but informative monologue about deferred annuities. The maitre d' hopped nervously and then headed for the kitchen.

Dr. Franks, for that is who the waiter really was, pulled up a chair.

"Where is the Lovely Henna this evening?"

"You stay away from me!" Dinky Dave slid further into the booth.

"Relax, Dink. I'm not here about that clunker you sold me." He took out a sheet of paper with the Antmen logo on it. "What can you tell me about this?"

Dinky Dave did his best not to look at the paper. He threw his head and arms around so much in an effort to look casual that the doctor thought he might pass out before answering.

"What? The Mighty Antmen Club?"

"It goes by another name, doesn't it? The Societas Homoformicidae.

"I don't know nothing about that."

He wasn't even trying to look casual now. Dr. Franks pushed him.

"Tell me about the missing men. The missing little men.

"I can't. He'll—he would kill me."

"Who? Who would kill you?"

Dinky Dave looked around wildly. "You know," he whispered at last. "You know him. At least, he knows you."

"Who?"

"The professor."

Dinky Dave suddenly relaxed. The doctor thought it was because he had come clean, but it was really because the maitre d' had returned from the kitchen with a large Samoan dishwasher.

"Stay away from me!" Dave called as Dr. Franks was dragged away. "And my Ford dealership! Definitely don't go there tonight."

Back outside, his pride wounded but his hat somewhat intact, Dr. Franks headed in the general direction of home. It was 8:30. Scrabble club had already started and he didn't like showing up half-way through a round; however, he was restless and didn't want to turn in just yet.

Passing over the George Washington Bridge into Gramercy Park, Dr. Franks wandered in the general direction of the Flatiron Building and soon found himself at the one place the car dealer made of point of telling him told not to go—Dinky Dave Ford on West 42nd. It was closed, but two new sedans were displayed in the front window on raised, tilted stages. It was on one of those angled platforms he first saw his ill-fated '52 Crown Vic. Bile inched up his throat, and he started to move on. Passing the alley, he heard a soft cry. He looked, but could see little in the darkness. But again, the cry.

"Help. Please." Almost a whisper.

Dr. Franks entered carefully. Midway into the alley there was a dark shape on the cobblestones near the wall.

"Help."

It was a man, laying face down. Dr. Franks tried to help him up, but there was resistance.

"I'm stuck," the man said.

The doctor now saw that the man was indeed stuck in a basement window. Grabbing him by the collar, he pushed open the window with a foot and pulled him out. Dr. Franks was not surprised to see that the man was short. In fact, he looked to be one of the little men from the library, complete with an oversized gray suit, which was now streaked with dirt and grease. But, the man was unable or unwilling to talk, beyond his initial cry for help.

The doctor took him to a nearby coffee shop in West 171st St. where the poor fellow, despite his size, wolfed down two club sandwiches and a slice of banana cream pie.

After a few rounds of coffee, Dr. Franks introduced himself.

"My name is Stanley O'Toole," the man replied. "I've just escaped from the Professor."

SOCIETAS HOMOFORMICIDAE

"All I wanted to do was buy a car," the diminutive O'Toole said. "Now I'm not even human. I'll never be able to buy off the rack again."

Dr. Franks let the man talk himself out, passing the time by ripping open sugar packets in preparation for his next refill. The man was raving—obviously suffering from *after-the-fact panic response*—and desperate to vent. Two refills came before O'Toole was calm enough for interrogation.

"Let's start at the beginning. How did you first hear about the Societas Homoformicidae?"

O'Toole pushed the parsley around his plate. "Like I said—when I bought my Ford Custom from Dinky Dave. He tells me I look like a savvy guy who wants to improve his lot in life. Tells me about the Mighty Antmen Club. A self-improvement program. Positive thinking. Special vitamins. The whole bill of goods."

The doctor raised a wooly eyebrow. "Vitamins?"

"More like a magic potion. I mean, look at me. I'm ruined."

O'Toole threw his arms out. Dr. Franks saw nothing unusual about the man, save that his pupils were dilated and his grimy jacket was about four sizes too large.

162

"Don't get me wrong. The program produced results. I felt more confident, especially with the ladies. And stronger. But at what cost, I ask you? At what cost?"

The waitress looked up from counting her tips. O'Toole's last comment had nearly been a shout. The doctor waved a hand at him to quiet him down.

"I think we're getting ahead of ourselves. Dinky Dave introduced you to this, uh, Mighty Antmen Club. Now–did he charge you anything for it?"

"Through the nose."

The waitress cleared their plates. O'Toole asked for another piece of pie and gave the waitress a friendly slap on the tush. The waitress reciprocated with a quick slap to the head.

"See? It's like I can't help myself?" He shook his head vigorously. "What was I saying?"

"Through the nose."

"Yeah. He charged us plenty. But like I said it was producing results. At first, we'd meet once, twice a week for training. Weights, confidence building, etiquette. Trips to the library to read Dale Carnegie books. Soon, he sells me an exclusive membership to the secret society.

"Societas Homoformicidae."

"Bingo. And I get even stronger. Drinking those supplements and whatnot. Then, before you know it you're spending all your time there. Your money is gone, your life is gone. Nothing is important to you except pleasing the Professor."

"Flekeman!"

O'Toole's pie arrived. One hand reached out to pinch her, but he restrained it with the other.

"I don't know his name. We called him the Professor. Short blonde guy zipping around with a cane." He waved a forkful of whipped cream for emphasis. "Except it ain't no cane, if you get me."

"I don't."

"It's like we were all hypnotized. Those supplements, I bet. And then came those tests." He shivered. "Those horrible tests. And the experiments." He wolfed down the rest of the pie. "Maybe it didn't work on me as well as the other guys. Whatever. I stopped taking the magic potion. And then today—after who knows how many—I'm sort of myself. I see the basement window and when no one's looking I bolt. And that's when you found me. And here we are."

Dr. Franks thoughtfully shook a few packets.

"And you don't know any more about this Professor?"

"Only that he's got something big planned for Sunday night. Calls it his Manhattan Project. Something involving *Toast of the Town.*"

"*Toast of the Town?* You mean Ed Sullivan's show?" Dr. Franks was having a hard time following the conversation. O'Toole's train of thought seemed to have jumped the track. "It's just called *The Ed Sullivan Show* now."

"Exactly."

Dr. Franks frowned. It wasn't much to go on. Also, the man had eaten the last of the pie.

"Is there anything else you can tell me? Anything at all?"

O'Toole barely shrugged. "Wait—there's this." He reached into his vest pocket and pulled out a battered leather notebook. "It's the Professor's journal. Funny, it was just lying there by the open window."

The doctor opened it, leafed through it. The writing was spidery and in a modified form of pig Latin. He thought he could decipher it.

"Thanks, O'Toole."

O'Toole said nothing. Dr. Franks noticed that the man's eyes were damp. His face a mask of sorrow.

"What am I gonna do, mister? I'm ruined. Ruined."

"Cheer up," the doctor said tersely. Emotional outbursts made him uneasy. "Surely you can start a new life. Get a job."

"A job?" O'Toole said, almost shouting again. "A job?" He opened his jacket.

"Who's gonna hire me like this?"

Dr. Franks tried to hide his shock. Sprouting out of the little man's sides, at about kidney level, were two black appendages with spiky hairs. Like legs of a tarantula. Or an ant. Down the aisle, a dinner plate shattered.

"I don't know," the doctor said after he recovered himself. "Um, can you fry an egg?"

O'Toole brightened a bit.

"Theoretically."

FLEKEMAN'S JOURNAL (SECRETS REVEALED)

Back in his mother's basement, Dr. Franks examined Professor Flekeman's notebook:

Ince-say is-thay is-ay ay-may irst-fay a-day in-ay e-thay ew-Nay orld-Way....

Luckily, he could translate it as he went along.

May 22, 1951. Since this is my first day in the New World I thought I'd start a new notebook. Also, most of my old notes were lost at the end of the war. But that's old news. Like all immigrants, I'm looking forward starting fresh here in America. My tabula, as they say, is rasa. I should say we, as I am anticipating the arrival of the Lovely Henna sometime this summer.

May 24, 1951. Boy, New York is a big city! The movies just don't do it justice. I took a bus tour and saw all the famous spots: Grand Central Station, the Empire State Building, Rockefeller Center, Broadway. Sorry to see that the Hippodrome is gone, though. Had lunch at the Carnegie Deli (who can eat that much corned beef?—I got a doggie bag). Went to Coney Island yesterday. Rather cool, but I guess that's not unusual this time of year in "The Big Apple." I suppose I should be saving my money what with the problems accessing my Swiss accounts. But I needed a few days off after that horrible month on the tramp steamer and all that mess with the Nazis. I mean, I thought I was evil, but those people– No, I can't think about that right now. Have to make plans for the future.

Sept. 5, 1951. Can't believe summer's over and I didn't make one entry in this journal! Where does the time go? More complications accessing my money made it necessary to get a job. And since I'm not exactly documented I had to take a menial janitorial job. Ah, for the halcyon days in Buenos Aires after the war where I had a modest mansion and a staff of twenty. Why did I ever leave? Oh, that's right–that pesky Simon Wiesenthal. What a pest, and me not even a Nazi. Not officially, at least.

Which only reminds me of the whole Mittelwerk fiasco. Okay, maybe creating a race of elephant/human hybrids was untenable (though I still maintain they would have had great attributes like strength, size and eidetic memory). But der Fuehrer wanted spider-men. At least that's what that meddling Colonel Kapukt kept telling me. I told them, I told them spiders were no good, not being communal creatures. And as I predicted we ended up having to knock them off the cavern walls with fire hoses. They were strong and devious, to be sure, but impossible to control. All I can say is I feel sorry for any folken who wander into the Harz Mountains without a big can of bug spray. But I can hardly be held accountable for that situation, any more than I can for the terrible things that happened to the workers. I was just doing what I was paid to do.

So now all of a sudden I'm an evil scientist, reviled on five continents (and probably Australia when you think about it). And for what? Furthering the cause of science? Making a few volunteers shoot webs out of their butts? What about the Americans–they dropped atomic bombs for goodness sake!

And to make matters worse, I'm junior janitor at the Flatiron Building.

Well, if everyone thinks I'm a villain then I'll be the best villain ever. As soon as I get hold of my money.

Still awaiting the arrival of the Lovely Henna, by the way. She says she needs a little more time in Switzerland to recuperate from the reconstructive surgery. I received a photo, though, and I think she looks lovely. Better than before, even, especially around the eyes and nose.

In other news, both the Yankees and the Giants are looking good. I'm hoping for a subway series!

October 10, 1951. Damn Yankees!

Jan. 1, 1952. A new year and still no Lovely Henna. She remains in Geneva, spending my francs. I've asked her to at least mail me some cash but she's been very niggardly in that regard. And here I am cleaning toilets! She insists we have to be careful because of the Nazi hunters.

May 22, 1952. No Lovely Henna. No lovely money. No time for my research. And on top of that I got turned down for a raise at work. Mr. Harris says he doesn't like my "attitude." I'm a mop jockey, how does attitude factor into my performance? What–am I supposed to walk around grinning like an idiot? I've got to get some funding. If not from my Swiss accounts, then somewhere local.

May 24, 1952. So tired of that street vendor putting sauerkraut on my frankfurter just because of my accent. I'm Belgian–not German! And no mayo for the fries–what's with that!?

December 26, 1952. Am I evil by design or choice? If it's the former I'm not really evil because I can't help myself. If it's the latter–by choice–well, I don't see how I could have made any other choice. What was I supposed to do? Spend my whole life in Africa studying those dreary vole people? No, I had to sign up with the Nazis and work on that spider-man project.

And I guess that means I'm not really evil. Okay, maybe evil-ish.

I know I haven't kept up with this journal. Been uber-busy with my research. That's right, I quit my janitorial job and found a patron! It's funny how it came about too.

I was reading the evening papers and who do I see a photo of but young Bernie Franks! Wendell's son. Except he's not so young anymore. Man, has he gotten fat (he couldn't get much stupider). Imagine my surprise at seeing someone I thought I had killed in 1938 right there in the *Trib*. Apparently, he's made a minor name for himself as an inventor of kitchen gadgetry. (Big whoop–I made spider-men!) The article was about some tiff he got into with a Dinky Dave, owner of the biggest Ford dealership in Manhattan. Franks claimed this Dave sold him a bad car, then they got into some kind of melee, and the result is young Franks has to stay away from the guy. One quote attributed to Dinky Dave especially caught my eye: "I didn't become incredibly rich by letting customers return vehicles."

There's no other way to describe it–it was an epiphany! I'm sitting there–September, early afternoon–gnawing on some rye bread before beginning the second shift. The sun was low over Hoboken and chose that moment to dip under the building's awning and zap me in the eyes. This guy, Dinky Dave, would be my patron! A man who was greedy enough to see the financial potential in my work, and morally flexible enough not to sweat the details. And, to add serendipity to synchronicity, Dr. Franks, the only man who might possibly muck up my fairly diabolical plan, isn't allowed anywhere near the guy.

I approached him carefully at first, feigning interest in one of his ghastly Detroit jalopies before revealing just enough of my research to get him hooked. The 35mm of those spider-men jumping around the V2s intrigued him. Of course I didn't tell him the full extent of my plans–he thinks I'm working on a muscle-building program. It also didn't hurt that he met the Lovely Henna.

Yes! Did I mention? Henna is here! As beautiful and statuesque as I imagined. Once I told her of the potential funding she flew right over. Funny what money does to a woman.

Dec. 26, 1953. Exactly one year since the last entry. It's been a busy year! The underground laboratory is complete. No one will ever know what horrors are hidden beneath Dinky Dave Ford until it is too late. Dink himself is proving more troublesome than anticipated, always nosing around and asking questions. I've asked the Lovely Henna to distract him.

February 2, 1954, Groundhog's Day. What silly holidays these Americans have!

Dink has been less of a problem. He's taken a shine to the Lovely Henna (who wouldn't?), even making her a model in his ridiculous television commercials. At least he's staying out of the laboratory. But he keeps asking when we will see some results. He doesn't seem to understand that this is interspecies biology I'm working on and not bucket seats!

The good news is that I have chosen an animal. Specifically, an insect. More specifically, the ant. I had dabbled with bees, termites and other communal species, but they all had their drawbacks. You can imagine what a 150-pound termite can do to your paneling. And voles were never even in the running. So—ants it is.

March 8, 1954. Making rapid progress on the ant/human hybrid. Of course I laid a lot of the groundwork in Africa and Germany. The key is not grafting or chemical in nature, but a combination of the two. I've developed a cocktail of formic acid and lysergic acid diethylamide, with a touch of cinnamon to taste. It dims the conscious mind while stimulating the insectoid areas of the medulla. The result is a subject who is both open to commands and determined to carry them out. It also comes in mint flavor.

One curious side effect is an enhancement of the libido. These guys just love the ladies. As a result, I've switched exclusively to smaller male subjects, who are easier to control (and restrain when necessary).

I am also rapidly working the bugs (no pun intended) out of the grafting procedure. I have developed a process for growing appendages to scale. Now all that remains is some simple surgery.

Of course I haven't told Dinky Dave about the grafting. Unfortunately, his interest in the Lovely Henna has not eliminated his requests for results. He's excited about the "ant elixir," as he calls it, and wants to start peddling the stuff as some kind of cure for impotence.

May 30, 1954. Spent a lovely weekend with the Lovely Henna in the Pine Barrens. I don't like to be away from the lab, but I needed some rest. Imagine my relief when I got back and found that the sedatives I had given the subjects had kept them from getting into trouble in my absence. I love my little minions, but they do get into mischief. The only pall on the weekend was the Lovely Henna's standoffishness. Maybe she's spending too much time with Dinky Dave.

Happy to report that the grafting experiments have gone well. Five of the first four subjects seem to be adapting. The fifth, named Tool or something—well, I don't know about that guy.

Also happy to report that Dink is off my back for now. I gave him a batch of the ant cocktail to do with as he will. He's started a secret society (my idea) called the Societas Homoformicidae (also my idea—like that half-wit would know Latin). First, he ropes people into something he calls the Mighty Antmen Club then, when they're hooked, he charges an exorbitant membership fee to get in the ultra-exclusive Societas. As long as he keeps things on the "low-down" it's fine with me. What's the worst that could happen, anyway? Some shrimp gets fresh with a waitress or pulls a muscle trying to open a pickle jar? Meanwhile, I'm making headway on my master plan. I'm calling it the Manhattan Project. Clever, huh?

Because that was what the Americans called their atomic bomb program and I'm here in Manhattan.

July 4, 1954. What is it with these Americans and their g— damned holidays? These firecrackers are working my minions into a frenzy. And as usual the Lovely Henna is nowhere to be found when I need her.

September 14, 1954. This time the Lovely Henna was around—and I did need her. I had an accident involving a circular saw and lost the use of my left leg. The only fix was to graft one of the appendages to my posterior (unlike the subjects, who get two anterior grafts). I now have what I refer to as a "third leg." The procedure has rendered me faster and more agile than before, if about two feet shorter. The only real negative is that Dink and the Lovely Henna snicker every time I say "third leg." Don't know what that's about.

December 26, 1954. How time flies! Sixteen years ago I was stuck in East Africa, giving tests to mouse people. Now I am on the verge of implementing my master plan. The minions are fully trained: strong, obedient and very polite. There are a few shirkers, but I'll deal with them.

I love the day after Christmas. The presents have been opened, the guests have gone, and one can finally relax. As I sit here in my subterranean lair, sipping peppermint schnapps and listening to Perry Como, I consider all those people I'm going to take revenge on. Am I evil? I guess so. But better me taking over the world than those commies.

Another note: Dink tells me he's having trouble controlling his little Antmen club. I suggested he reduce the dosage and close membership. I hope there's no trouble from that quarter. At least until my plans are complete.

When Dr. Franks finally looked up it was well past midnight. The journal had answered many questions, but raised a few more. What was the crazy loon planning, what exactly was his Manhattan Project? And how did Ed Sullivan figure into it?

He had less than forty-eight hours to figure it out.

DINKY DAVE FORD

The next afternoon, Saturday, Sven the mechanic walked briskly into the service department of Dinky Dave Ford, just a few blocks east of the Flatiron Building. His blue jumpsuit was set off by a brown tam and a prominent coffee stain at the curve of his abdomen. Sven was large, with a regal bearing and a tool case that looked suspiciously like a tackle box. He was almost past the service desk when the manager noticed him.

"Hey mac–where do you think you're going?"

Sven spun around on the heels of his Hush Puppies.

"I am Sven the Svede vot fixes the foreign wee-hicles," he said.

The manager scratched his head. "Sven? Foreign wee–? Oh, you mean imported cars."

"Ya. I vas tolt you had a wee-hicle vot needs the service. Perhaps a Sa-ab or the Wol-wo."

"The only foreign car we got is Dinky Dave's Mercedes."

"Da. The Mercedes," Sven said quickly. "A fine Svedish wee-hicle. I must transfuse mitz the oil."

Sven shifted from one foot to the other, producing a tinkling of glass from inside the tackle box. The manager eyed Sven like a husband eyes a dish prepared by his wife from a

174

recipe in *Good Housekeeping*. One that involves Brussels sprouts. He was about to speak when the phone rang.

"It's around the back," he said as he picked up the receiver. "And you're on your own. The service department closes in five minutes."

"Da," said Sven, producing an oversized wrench from his pocket. "I fix myself. I fix goot!"

Once around the corner, Sven removed his jaunty tam, allowing anyone who saw him to realize he was in reality the famous Dr. Franks, explorer, philanthropist and inventor of the knife-sharpening thing on the back of the electric can opener. The Mercedes was easy to spot, a bright red machine parked in a far corner. He crossed to it quickly. The gentle tinkling of glass in the tackle box told him his portable formic acid testing kit was now a random collection of Pyrex shards. He would have to go by taste. No—that was for folic acid. He made a mental note to make a written note of the difference.

Two mechanics from a nearby hallway headed for the exit in the back. The doctor's timing had been perfect. The showroom was closed by noon on Saturday. He had only to wait until the service department had cleared out to begin snooping around.

He struck what he hoped was a thoughtful mechanic pose, stroking his chin and throwing in a frown for good measure. Dr. Franks understood thoroughly the workings of the internal combustion engine. It was, by engineering standards, a fairly simple machine. He would have no trouble making a show of checking the plugs and fluids. What never failed to stymie him, however, was opening the hood.

After some trial and error and a few subtle smacks with the wrench, he had the bonnet up. In no time at all wires and hoses were strewn randomly about the engine cavity. It looked exactly like a car in the middle of a repair. That or vandalism.

The last of the mechanics had departed, but he waited another half hour just to be safe. Then he headed down the long hall to the showroom. Since it doubled as a television studio, it was separated from the offices and garage by two sets of doors. The first set was open, but the second locked. He easily picked it with one of the numerous hairpins he kept on his person. A trick he learned from Houdini.

The doctor found himself in a large area separated from the rest of the showroom by a thick red curtain. A state-of-the-art television camera was stationed on one end. Opposite it, perched on the rotating ramp made famous in the Dinky Dave commercials, rested a purple and white two-tone Crown Victoria with a tinted roof panel.

Dr. Franks felt a twinge of anger as he surveyed the gorgeous vehicle. It reminded him of the way Dinky Dave had ripped him off and made him look like the bad guy. But he told himself to focus; he wasn't here for revenge, but to look for clues.

And he noticed a big one right off the bat. The Crown Victoria had rolled partway off the display ramp. A yard in front of its beautifully designed concave grille was Dinky Dave's pinky ring, the one with the logo of the Societas Homoformicidae. Inserted through the ring was Dinky Dave's pinky, which was attached to the object that had prevented the car from rolling completely off the ramp—Dinky Dave.

The body was face up, with the legs and most of the torso under the car itself. It looked exactly as if Dinky Dave had tried—and failed—to lift the Crown Vic. The doctor checked the body. No pulse, no respiration. The body was still warm, which meant he had died recently. Possibly after the showroom closed at noon.

At first, Dr. Franks was frozen by shock and confusion. This was the last thing he expected. Absentmindedly, he leaned against the passenger door and lit up a Turkish Dandy.

Dinky Dave's death, like his torso, was quite a twist. He had intended to sneak into the dealership and, from there, find a way into Flekeman's underground lab. Now he supposed he would have to call Inspector Grimes, which would put him in a tough spot since he trespassing and violating a restraining order.

As he took a long drag his luck changed, though he could never afterward determine in which direction. Suddenly the harsh lighting flickered on and he heard the same dreaded *step-step-click* from the other day. A short blonde man with a cane skittered quickly up to him.

"Professor Flekeman."

"The celebrated Dr. Franks. What an intriguing surprise."

The doctor reached for the wrench in his pocket, but before he could pull it out, six of the professor's minions rushed him from behind and held him immobile. Their pincer grips, although clumsy, were vice-like.

Flekeman approached. "I am amazed, doctor. How did you know I was here?"

Dr. Franks nodded at the corpse. "The symbol on Dinky Dave's ring."

He examined the Belgian doctor. The man was not a true albino, just horribly pale. His face, which Dr. Franks had originally thought youthful, was nearly devoid of features due to numerous cosmetic surgeries. The skin was taut and smooth like a pudding. His thin lips barely moved when he spoke. He did, however, have pretty eyes.

"How sad about Dinky," Flekeman said. "Still, he served his purpose."

Dr. Franks struggled to free himself, but whenever he shook off one antman two more took his place.

"Why did you kill him?" he demanded. "And what do you have to do with these deaths? And the Societas Homoformicidae?"

Flekeman emitted a short, derisive laugh.

"Yes, yes. You have the pieces, Dr. Franks, but you can't quite fit them together." He ran a skeletal finger across the hood of the car and then seemed to come to a decision. "But where are my manners? Now that you are here I must show you my work. I've made much progress since my days in Africa. Again, I apologize for throwing you off the mountain."

Flekeman turned off the lights and led Dr. Franks down a flight of stairs. The antmen had released him but followed too closely to allow any chance of escape.

After a long descent they arrived at a cavernous room. The nearest half was set up like a banquet facility: rows of tables with scores of place settings. The far end was a workout area. Antmen scurried about both areas. None bothered to look up as the newcomers entered.

Flekeman made a dramatic sweep with his arm. "This is my Manhattan Project. A mighty army of antmen!"

"Hmph. They seem a bit clumsy," Dr. Franks said, for he had noticed the table tops were a mess. The tablecloths were stained with wine and gravy, and the antmen seemed to be having trouble manipulating the utensils and stemware.

Noticing the disarray, Flekeman balled his little fists and let loose with a string of Flemish epitaphs.

"Yes," he said between clenched teeth. "The new appendages are not as precise as I had hoped. But what they lack in delicacy they make up for in brute strength. You may return to your training, gentlemen."

The antmen escort dispersed and joined the others. Flekeman led Dr. Franks farther into the room.

"And here they are. My antmen."

Dr. Franks nodded. Each minion had an extra pair of arms protruding from his abdomen. Insect arms with claw-like hands that could be hidden under the baggy jackets when not in use.

"They are mighty. But they are also, I hope, gentlemen. Hence, the training in etiquette—darn it guys, the fish fork goes outside the salad fork!—I would like to think I am not totally evil."

They reached the workout area. Dozens of antmen were lifting barbells—hundreds of pounds—with their insect arms. Dozens more were dropping them, often on their own toes. Flekeman rolled his eyes and quickly escorted Dr. Franks away from the scene.

"I have also improved on my work from ten years ago, when I was in the employ of the Nazis."

Dr. Franks frowned. "Yes. I read your journal."

Flekeman raised an eyebrow—the one that wasn't frozen in place. "Did you? I had hoped that Tool fellow would give it to you. Oh, did you think you found him by accident? But come—we will have a drink and I will answer all your questions."

Flekeman began to lead Dr. Franks to his office.

"And then you will kill me, right?" the doctor said.

It was time for action and Dr. Franks took it. He made a dash for the stairs. But before he got halfway across the floor Flekeman had overtaken him.

"I do not need my antmen to keep you here, doctor. For I am myself an antman."

Flekeman pulled off his coat. Dr. Franks saw what he knew to be the "third leg" from Flekeman's diary: a pneumatic piston with a wooden shoe on the end. It was short—about the length of what Dr. Franks now saw were two shortened flesh-and-blood legs. And just below his right arm was a mechanical arm. He was asymmetrical, but technically had six appendages.

"Crude yet effective. I am as fast and agile as a greyhound thanks to my third leg—why does everyone find that so funny?"

The doctor stopped giggling.

THE ANTMEN

The two enemies sat opposite each other in Flekeman's office/laboratory. Books, beakers and chop suey cartons lay haphazardly about. A large and heavily marked-up map of the Tri-State area adorned one wall. On the other, a caricature of the professor and the Lovely Henna as cowboys. Dr. Franks declined the offer of port.

"First," Flekeman said, "let me applaud your homoscientific skills."

"Me? I failed to solve the case."

"Yes, but you knew something more was going on. The cards. The acid residue. The manner of the suicides."

"So. They were suicides?"

Flekeman's mouth pinched itself into a tight, tiny line.

"That fool Dinky Dave! His greed overcame his patience. He sold too many memberships to the society. The cards, the logo—those were his ideas. Well, the name was mine, but you know..." He tossed some packets of soy sauce into the trash. "Then he gave his members too much of the formula. It made them crazy: sex-crazed and aggressive. Some—the editor, the choir director, the bookkeeper, the clown—were fatalities."

"Sad."

"Certainly! The investigation almost ruined my plans. You of all people should understand the difficulties with a project such as mine. I have taken milquetoasts, men small of body and mind, neglected by society and rejected by the fairer sex—toll booth collectors, government clerks, proofreaders—and reconditioned them. And of those, only the best candidates have received the grafted appendages."

"And Dinky Dave?"

There was a loud crash of dishes from downstairs. Flekeman rolled his eyes.

"He was becoming troublesome. Thought he was a partner because he provided funds and a location for my project. But I am not a man to share power."

"I see."

"Also, he was trying to steal my girlfriend."

Dr. Franks raised an eyebrow.

"The Lovely Henna."

"Yes. We've been together a long time. Seventeen years. One would hardly recognize her if one knew her in 1938."

Flekeman raised his good eyebrow again. Dr. Franks didn't understand the point the professor was making so he changed the subject.

"And this Manhattan Project of yours? What is it? Are you planning to take over the world?"

"No. That would be crazy. I'm going to take over *The Ed Sullivan Show.*"

"Yes, The Ed Sullivan Show. That new Ed Sullivan show. What is the purpose of that?"

"I will hold him ransom. Along with Steve & Edie and Carmen Basillio. And maybe a dog act if it's any good. I will demand a million dollars and the *Queen Elizabeth II.*"

Dr. Franks shifted in his seat. As an avid reader of train and cruise ship schedules he knew the *RMS QEII* was currently docked in New York harbor for an upgrade (including shuffleboard courts and shag carpeting). "So that you can take your antmen to some island and continue your research."

"Then, when we are ready, we will take over the world." Flekeman looked off wistfully. "I'm thinking Aruba. White sand beaches...rum drinks. Plus, it would be good for their economy." He shrugged. "I do what I can."

Dr. Franks hesitated. He was in a tight spot.

"And...this would be tomorrow night's show?"

"Yes. Sunday night."

"And where would you be staging your army? I mean, you can't simply meet at Grand Central Station."

"We are borrowing a building two blocks from CBS studio. The Flatiron Building." Flekeman stood up. "Now. Have I answered all your questions? No loose ends to tie up in your mind?"

Dr. Franks rose slowly.

"So the dead men were simply unintended casualties in an insane plan to take Ed Sullivan hostage, acquire a boat, go to an island and then prepare take over the world?" He shook his head up and down, then sideways. "You really are one mad scientist."

"But not totally evil, I hope."

There was a clank of metal, followed closely by a cry of pain.

"Excuse me, doctor. I must attend to my minions."

They stepped outside.

"And you're not going to kill me?"

"I was going to, but I'd hate you to think poorly of me. Anyway, who's going to believe you?"

Dr. Franks rose carefully.

"So I'm free to go."

"Of course. Thank you for stopping by."

"You lured me here simply to explain your crazy plan to me?"

"What can I say? I'm a people person."

Dr. Franks walked to the stairway. No one stopped him. He made his way carefully up to the dark studio.

A tall figure awaited him. The Lovely Henna.

"The famous Dr. Franks," she purred.

A thousand thoughts came to him. Why was she there? Had she seen Dinky Dave's body? Would she try to help him or stop him? What kind of calisthenics did she do to get those gams? And what about Flekeman's cryptic references to her: the coma, the surgery, their seventeen-year relationship? Seventeen years ago the professor was in Tanganyika, in the Usambara Mountains with the mysterious vole people. That was where his father had fallen to his death, where he himself would have met his end had the vole people and the laughing porters at the base of the mountain not found him and carried him to back to civilization. And Gertrude—

The Lovely Henna approached the doctor, put an elegant finger to his lips.

"It's been a long time. Do you recognize me?"

He looked her up and down. She was striking but not familiar. And yet—

No. The nose was wrong.

Then he remembered the journal: the plastic surgery.

"Gertrude?"

Her eyes, no longer squinty but still pale and weak, brightened at the name.

"Bernard!"

"You—you're here!" he stuttered. It was impossible, like someone breaking Babe Ruth's home run record or an actor being elected President.

"When you left I had no choice but to go with Flekeman."

"I didn't leave. I was tossed off the mountain."

"He's a great man." Henna pushed her body against his. "Remember how I said I wanted a great man?"

The warmth of her body, especially the jiggly parts, left him speechless.

"There was an accident during the war, Bernie. I was left in a coma."

She ran a hand through his hair, which the doctor had slicked back to look Swedish. She wiped off the grease on his shoulder.

"All those years in that coma. Bernie—I dreamed of you."

She traced the coffee stain on his overalls with her fingers. He shivered.

"But I never heard from you."

"Were you listed?"

One of her hands inched down slowly.

"I had no choice but to go with Flekeman."

He mumbled something incoherent.

"He's a nice man. Remembers birthdays."

Franks heard his voice say, "But he's evil."

She reached into his hip pocket. He gasped.

Her eyes flashed with anger. "At least he's done something with his life!"

He felt a terrific pain at the base of his skull. As he blacked out he realized he had been whacked with his own wrench.

THE HOSPITAL

Sergeant Marvin Dingle found himself on a beautiful Pacific island, walking barefoot on a warm sand beach at sunset–yet the sun didn't get in his eyes nor the sand in his underwear. His wife, glowing with beauty, eyes wide with love and admiration, walked by his side and never opened her mouth except to kiss his hand with her full cherry lips. Trailing behind them was his stunningly white herd of Australian sheep and, behind them, Inspector Grimes, who was hoping Dingle would deign to offer advice on an important homicide case. As the sun set they arrived at a large pavilion, lit with torches and filled with admirers. Everyone–men, women and sheep–dined on a lavish meal paid for by the proceeds from Dingle's laundrovendoramamat. Shiny nickels, dimes and quarters were stacked everywhere. Later, he would give a viola concert. It was a wonderful, magical island where everyone thought Dingle was brilliant and all his crazy plans came to fruition and he never got run over by taxis or fell down stairwells. Then a nurse accidentally kicked out his morphine drip and he was back in Bed 2, Room 1634 of the Bronx Hospital in Midtown Manhattan.

Over in Bed 1, Dr. Franks knew even before opening his eyes, from the smell of dead skin and toilet cleaner that he was in the hospital again. It was not a surprise, happening as it did at least once during every case.

A dull arc of pain caromed through his skull. The life of a homoscientist was not an easy one. Perhaps in years to come, he thought, they would do television shows about brave crime-fighting scientists like him. The characters would wear tailored shirts, have nice hair and work in futuristic offices with plenty of backlighting. There would be catchphrases. But for now all he got for his trouble was a concussion.

Cotton filled his mouth. At least it felt that way. Did he indeed have rabies on top of everything else? He reached for the glass of water on the table in front of him, but something prevented his reaching it. He was handcuffed to the bed.

"Oh, you're awake," Inspector Grimes said, eyeing him suspiciously. "Can I get you some water?"

"No thanks." Suddenly, he wasn't thirsty. Weren't those the cardinal symptoms of rabies—thirst and lack of it? "Am I under arrest? It's for violating the restraining order, right?"

"I wouldn't worry about that."

"Great—because I've cracked the case."

"Oh, have you?" Grimes said. He took out his notepad and a pen.

"Dinky Dave. I always knew he was no good. He was involved with that Professor Flekeman to create a race of superhuman antmen."

"Antmen, you say?" Inspector Grimes said as he scribbled. "Again with the ants."

"The accountant, the choir director and his organ, the editor, the actor—they were failed experiments in a fiendish plot to take over the world. Starting with Ed Sullivan."

"You, ah, really don't like Dinky Dave."

"He screwed me over," Dr. Franks said between head throbs. "But that has nothing to do with this case."

"You're sure of that?"

Dr. Franks paused for a moment to let his head clear.

"There's something you're not telling me, isn't there?"

"Several things."

Dr. Franks took a deep breath and let it out slowly. The patient behind the curtain in Bed 2 started moaning. A nurse entered with a large hypodermic needle and soon his roommate was mumbling about sheep.

"Go ahead," Dr. Franks said at last. "I can take it."

Inspector Grimes checked his notes.

"First, your mother called. She said she'll be by to visit as soon as possible and that she threw out your tinker toys."

"My molecule!"

"Second, your cousin Phelps called and said you received another royalty check and he's already invested it and something about 'freaking Giants.'"

"My can opener money!"

"Third, your pet squirrel needs a heart operation."

"Dash!"

"Fourth, your days as a homoscientist for the New York Police Department are over for good."

"But what about all those cases I solved?"

"Franks, I never had the heart to tell you this, but you were wrong about all those cases. That man you said was shot by someone hanging upside-down to make it look like a self-inflicted gunshot wound? Turns out it *was* a self-inflicted gunshot wound. That guy found dead in a locked room with only a puddle of water and a rope? He hung himself by standing on a block of ice. Guess we should have realized that since it happened in an ice house."

"So I missed a few—"

"Fifth, Dinky Dave is dead."

"That I knew."

"He was killed about the time you were at the dealership. Which brings us to number six: You are under arrest for the murder of Dinky Dave."

"But the Lovely Henna—"

"Says you attacked her when she found you standing over Dinky Dave's body and was forced to defend herself."

Dr. Franks leaned back. "Remember when I said I could take the bad news? I changed my mind."

Inspector Grimes flipped through his notes. "Oh, but there is some good news!"

"Really?" Dr. Franks said, brightening.

"You're going to be a father! No wait—that's me. Hey, how about that?"

Later, as Dr. Franks drifted into a morphine-induced dream, he wondered, not for the last time, if he should have been a cobbler.

THE FLATIRON BUILDING

His mother was there. He could not see her, but he knew. She had grown from an annoying stick of a thing into a bloated monster, gray and covered with fur. "Bernie!" she cried as if from a distance. "Bernie, are you there?" In his mind's eye the amorphous creature shuddered, the face contorted, and then two antennae poked through the head and two claw-like arms exploded from the sides. "Bernie, are you there?" The creature clutched at its chest with its new appendages before collapsing. "Bernie. Bernie!"

Dr. Franks awoke. The sun had gone down, but there was light coming from the hospital corridor. The telephone receiver lay by his ear.

"Yes, mother. I'm listening," he said.

"I asked if you need anything."

Dr. Franks exhaled. His head didn't hurt quite so much. "What time is it?"

"Let me look. About 4:45."

Four forty-five? He felt around for his Turkish Dandies. They weren't on the table. And he was still handcuffed to the bed. And there was something he was forgetting. Something urgent.

"Are they feeding you? Don't forget to keep the plastic utensils. We can use them when taking guests."

"Mother, I have to go."

"You're in the hospital. Where do you have to go?"

Dr. Franks sat up. He felt loopy but otherwise okay.

"To Ed Sullivan's TV show. No. I mean, I have to call Gertrude. I mean Stella. Good night, mother."

He hung up. He dialed. As he waited, he tried to get his bearings. Flekeman and his antmen were going to attack Ed Sullivan, take him hostage along with a dog act. Flekeman said his army would meet at the Flatiron Building, which was two blocks from the studio. Most likely they would attack during the show. And the show started in less than three and a half hours.

"Hello?" Stella sounded anxious. "Oh doc, good to hear from you. How are the sawbones treating you?"

"Stella, I don't have time to explain. Can you and Cousin Phelps get down here as fast as possible? No, I don't need any magazines. Well, *Look* if you have it."

Dr. Franks didn't know how he would stop the antmen, but something would come to him. First, he had to deal with the cuffs. Fortunately, the authorities hadn't found the hairpin he kept in his nostril.

Once free, he tiptoed to the door. As he suspected, a police officer was sitting in a chair just outside (Dr. Franks was, after all, under arrest for murder). He got his clothes from the closet and put them on as quietly as possible. Then he slipped back into bed and pulled the sheet up to his neck.

Stella arrived at 5:30, armed with magazines and flowers.

"What took you so long?" Dr. Franks demanded.

"You're welcome, doc!" she said. She put the gifts on the dresser.

"Where's Phelpsy?"

"Right here." Cousin Phelps entered, followed closely by Einstein.

"What's he doing here?" the doctor demanded.

"Are you kidding? He's been downstairs ever since they brought you in." Phelps grabbed the Look magazine and started paging through it. "What's this I hear about you getting arrested, doc?"

"What's this I hear about the freaking Giants?" the doctor fired back.

Stella examined Dr. Franks' bandaged head. "Ooo, that's quite a goose egg."

The doctor pushed her back and slowly eased himself off the bed. Stella steadied him.

"There is absolutely no time to explain," he whispered, mindful of the policeman. "You all must do exactly what I ask of you. The fate of the city, the world, and definitely the island of Aruba depend on it."

Phelps and Stella started to protest, but he shushed them. Einstein, as always, was ready for anything. When the doctor had gained their consent, he pulled them close for a huddle.

"Phelpsy and Einstein, take Einstein's truck and go secure as much glue as you can. A few hundred gallons should suffice."

Phelpsy eyes popped. "Where are we supposed to get that much glue? On a Sunday night?"

"I'd try wherever rendering plant took our race horse," Dr. Franks said. "But first, we have to distract the guard and sneak me out."

Stella frowned. "Won't they notice that you're missing?"

Dr. Franks raised an eyebrow. "I've got a plan for that."

Sergeant Dingle was in Australia. His wife and daughter, now a rose-cheeked toddler, were happily riding around on kangaroos as Dingle played the viola. Then the ground began to shake. Something was wrong.

Dingle woke up. His bed had been moved to the other side of the room. And he was handcuffed to the railing.

"Mr. Franks," a voice said. "Mr. Franks. According to your chart you're running a fever. We're going to fix that with an ice bath followed by a cooling enema."

Dingle tried to inform the nurse of the error but found his mouth was bandaged shut. He sighed a muffled sigh. He wasn't in Australia anymore.

"Now doc, about the car."

The throbbing in Dr. Franks' head had increased to an audible thumping now that he had made the walk down the stairway and out the emergency room doors. Still, the amount of time he stood assessing Stella's vehicle seemed excessive.

"Is this a Crown Victoria?" he asked. His voice betrayed awe and accusation. The car was a black and white two-tone. Its tail fins and forward-slanted lines made it look like it was speeding even when in park.

"It's a '55," Stella admitted. "I didn't want to tell you. Thought you'd be mad."

He was mad. But he also needed a ride.

"Nonsense. I was just admiring the whitewalls."

Soon they were headed to the garment district, with Stella at the wheel.

"What's in the garment district?" she asked.

"Ace-Descent Laboratory Supply." Dr. Franks let out a sad little sigh. The crown vic still had that new car smell. "Are you any good at breaking and entering?"

"This is ridiculous," Cousin Phelps said.

Einstein didn't respond. The two were in his old pick-up, heading for the docks. Phelps had insisted on driving.

"I gotta see my bookie. I got a hot tip."

"No. We're getting glue."

Phelps looked sideways twice at Einstein, sizing him up. The man looked tiny, in spite of his stack of white hair. He was all crooked and had pop bottle glasses from years of reading in the dark of his newsstand. Phelps figured he could take him.

Seeing a subway station, he pulled over.

"Get your own glue," Phelps said, putting the clutch in neutral. "I'm going home."

He opened the door and started to slide out, but found that he couldn't move. Einstein had him by the scruff of the neck. He tried to break free but could not.

"I bet I move three tons of paper through my little newsstand every day," Einstein said, still looking forward. "How 'bout that?" He turned Phelps' face toward his own. "I don't want to let down the doc. And neither do you."

He let go. Phelps closed the door and brushed himself off.

"Sure. Sure. Glue it is."

TOAST OF THE TOWN

Backstage at the CBS studio a cadaverous man mumbled to himself. He knew the show would be fine. His shows were always fine. That was the beauty of having so many acts; if one bombed the next would kill. No, he wasn't worried about the show; he was worried about his own performance.

He checked himself in the mirror and frowned internally (the permanent, exterior frown on his waxen face never changed). No matter how much he paid for his suits, and how much he spent having them altered, they always looked like he had purchased the wrong size right off the rack.

The man personally knew many successful television personalities who looked much worse. George Jessel, for instance. But they all had talent or personality. His only talent was finding talent. He had to face facts: he was destined to be the worst host of the best show on television.

A troupe of Brazilian jugglers hurried by.

Still, he worked on each and every introduction. The standard ones didn't worry him: Topo Gigio, Jackie Vernon. You couldn't screw those up. Plus, he liked those acts. It was this new stuff, the rockabilly and the soul acts. They gave him fits. He wanted to showcase it; he just couldn't disguise the fact that he didn't get it. Like this Bo Diddley that Dr. Jive had brought him. He took a nice song like *Mockingbird* and just destroyed it with those screeching guitar noises. Despite that, he wanted to give the act a professional intro.

"Rolling, rocking? Rocking, rolling, jazzy?"

Just offstage, Carmen Basilio was shadow boxing. The poor punch-drunk bastard, the man thought. He checked his watch: fifteen minutes till show time.

"Stop laughing and help me out of here."

Dr. Franks was sitting, butt down, in a large box of safety goggles in the Ace-Descent Laboratory Supply showroom. The store was closed, but Stella picked the lock in less than a minute. ("Who doesn't know how to pick a lock, hon?") The Ed Sullivan Show was due to start in fifteen minutes.

"Here," Stella said. "Let me..."

"No. I'll just..."

"Why don't we...?"

"No! Not that way!"

The box fell slowly sideways, spitting the doctor out upright.

"Oh," he said, surprised. "Very good. Now—help me get the magnifying glass."

"Which one?" Stella looked around. The aisles were stacked nearly floor to ceiling with flasks, aprons, scales and other scientific equipment.

Dr. Franks pointed. "That one."

Standing in the display window, held up by two strands of nylon filament, stood the ten-foot-high magnifying glass. A four-foot-high divider separated it from the aisle.

"You'll have to climb up and unfasten it," Dr. Franks said. "I'm still a bit dizzy."

"Me?" Stella opened her arms, palms out. "I'm wearing a dress."

Dr. Franks stared. Not only did she have a crisp black floral print number but also a fashionable matching scarf tied over her hair. She reminded him of something.

"Why on earth are you wearing that?" he asked.

Her brows furrowed. "Well, I am a woman."

That's what she reminded him of. A woman.

He helped her over the divider and handed her a pair of needle nose pliers he found in a display. Soon they had the device out the door. It would have taken too long to tie it to the roof so Dr. Franks held it against the side. Stella turned the ignition.

"You owe me big time for this," she said. "Don't you think?"

Dr. Franks knew he should say something. She had been very nice, very helpful and very, very friendly in the short week he had known her. Perhaps, it slowly occurred to him, she had even dressed up for him.

"Um, those are dandy floor mats."

On the far side of the Flatiron Building from the CBS Studio 50 Theater, hundreds of tuxedo-clad men filtered quietly through the revolving door. Professor Flekeman watched from his perch on top of the security desk. The lone security guard, a wide, sedentary fellow, raised a questioning eyebrow.

"Busboy convention," the scientist explained.

The guard shrugged and went back to his crossword puzzle. He'd seen stranger.

Soon the entire antman army, four thousand strong, was inside. Little well-appointed men filled every floor, waiting patiently, clicking their dynamic new appendages. They had no thought but to obey their leader. And meet girls.

Flekeman hopped off the desk. It was nearly 6 p.m. Soon he would take all of New York by surprise, as well as taking them for a million dollars and the *RMS QEII*. And, once established in Aruba, it would be only a matter a years until he could take over the world. He surveyed his minions and nodded happily. The tuxedoes had been a nice touch.

"We'll wait until they get started, then head on over," he said to himself.

Suddenly, the guard looked up at him urgently.

"Hey mac–what's a four-word letter word for malevolent?"

Ellas Otha Bates, a young black man, loitered outside the CBS Studio 50 Theater. The show had already started, but there was still a large crowd outside. It would be his first time on the show, but that didn't intimidate him. Nor did the crowd. He'd seen bigger ones at the Apollo. Besides, they weren't here to see him. He was just filling in for some old comedy duo, Jerry and Jimmy or something.

He took a drag of his Winston and watched the searchlight cut a foggy beam across the autumn night. He flicked his smoke, being careful not to get ashes on his fur-collared jacket.

No, he was worried about his guitar. Specifically, its sound. The amps weren't his normal set and just didn't provide the oomph he wanted.

Bates' eyes followed the beam and noticed a silhouette, as if someone was trying to make a shadow puppet. He looked over at the searchlight and saw a sedan parked next to it. A large bearded man got out of the passenger side, struggling to hold what looked like a giant lollipop. He put out his cigarette and wandered over.

"Hey man, you need help?"

The bearded man looked Bates up and down.

"No. We'll park it ourselves, thank you."

Bates jerked his head back. "I'm not a valet!"

"Oh! I'm sorry. I didn't mean to assume that because you are ...because you...I mean, I have many friends who are–"

"Can you work a spotlight, hon?" Stella interrupted.

Bates thought a moment. "Theoretically."

Standing in the bed of the pick-up, Einstein swung a large hammer at a railroad spike and punctured a 55-gallon drum. When the clear, sticky contents began to ooze out, he signaled the driver.

"Slow, Phelpsy. Go slow."

Cousin Phelps jerked the truck into gear. The fluid spilled off the back, leaving a six-inch-wide trail on the street.

"How far do we go?"

"Twice around the building, or until it runs out," Einstein called. He looked back behind him. A block away was a crowd and a searchlight. "And hurry. But hurry slow."

"It's okay. It's for the show."

Bates was having enough trouble adjusting the searchlight without also having to convince the security guards to leave him alone.

"I'm Bo Diddley. I'm with the show. Go in and ask Dr. Jive if you don't believe me. Or Mr. Sullivan"

One of the guards ran off. The other stood several feet away, watching dubiously.

Dr. Franks and Stella were standing on top of Stella's Crown Vic (in their stocking feet, so as not to scratch the finish), balancing the magnifying glass.

"Turn it lower," the doctor yelled to Bates.

Bates swung the light down. The guy in the battered raincoat was obviously crazy. When he had asked him what he was doing, the man said, "Did you ever kill ants with a magnifying glass?" "That must be one hell of an ant," Bates had replied. The crazy man had just laughed, "It's an entire colony!"

But Bates figured, why not? It got his mind off amplifying his guitar. And he'd done wilder things growing up in Chicago.

When the beam was finally aligned with the glass it sent a focused ray right down the block. Now that was cool. It was like that ray gun from *War of the Worlds*. Bates could see, down where the ray was concentrated, a pick-up truck and two men waving frantically. Nearby, someone cursed.

"Shoot and darn!" Dr. Franks cried. "We need a stronger light."

The barrels were empty. Einstein and Phelps had made it two laps around the Flatiron Building, putting down a two-foot-wide swath of glue, plus a ten-foot-wide puddle between them and the studio.

"There's the doc!" Einstein cried.

Phelps could see his relative on top of a car in front of the theater, holding up what looked like a sheet of glass.

"Wave!" Einstein ordered.

He did, and a few seconds later, a beam of light shot through the glass and onto the glue in front of them. They jumped back.

"He's crazy!" Phelps said.

Einstein beamed. "He's a genius. See what's he's doing?"

They waited. But nothing happened.

Behind them, they heard a slow clapping. When they turned they saw a short pale man with a third leg.

"He truly is a genius," the man said calmly. "I had not expected to see Dr. Franks again. But no matter. It is too little. And it is too late."

Einstein and Phelps were speechless, not because of the man but because of what was approaching. An army of short men in baggy tuxedoes.

"Call the zoo," Phelps said. "The penguins have escaped."

Stella cupped her hands around her mouth and yelled.

"Run, you idiots!"

Down the street, Einstein and Phelps ran toward the line of glue. Einstein cleared it, but Phelps seemed stuck, because Einstein went back and began pulling on the other's arm. After a struggle, they moved away from the Flatiron Building, Phelps hobbling to keep up.

"I think he lost a shoe," Stella added. "Isn't it usually his shirt, doc?"

But Dr. Franks was gone. She looked around. He was nowhere.

"Hey lady!" Bates cried. "How long is this going to take? I got a show to do."

Stella looked down the street. The beam was focused correctly, as far as she knew, but what was the next step? Wasn't something supposed to happen?

"Just a few more seconds, Mr. Bates. Please."

Now she could see that a large group of men down the street approaching the shiny line. They stopped just short of it and milled about, uncertain.

Bates was joined by another bespectacled black man.

"Bo!" he said to Bates. "Get your butt in here!"

Dr. Franks ran up, dragging the end of a huge electrical cord.

"Found a Con Ed relay station," he explained.

Bates shook his head. He did like the crazy guy's style.

"Hold on, Dr. Jive," Bates said with a laugh. "We're burning ants."

Dr. Franks took off the panel on the side of the searchlight and started fiddling with the connections.

"Hey man—shouldn't you be grounded or something?"

Dr. Franks looked up. "Eh? What's that?"

There was a loud crack and the doctor flew in a backwards arc, landing hard on the pavement. The searchlight became too hot to touch and the beam doubled its intensity.

"Right," Dr. Franks said, patting out a small fire in his hair. "Grounded."

Down the block, Professor Flekeman stepped onto the loop of glue, his three boots barely sticking to the stuff.

"Foolish," he muttered. He gestured for his minions to follow.

Suddenly, the glue around him burst into flames. The fire ran swiftly in two directions, making a fiery V before turning down both corners to surround the Flatiron Building. The antmen, more ant than man at this point, panicked. They ran in all directions, bumping into each other until, leaderless and purposeless, they plunged into the fire.

Einstein and Phelps watched from a safe distance. Einstein shielded his face from the heat. The creatures, now humanoid torches, waved and emitted high-pitched cries. But one word, bellowed repeatedly by one enraged voice, nearly drowned them out. "Franks!" it raged, "Franks!"

"You know what?" Phelps said at last. "Suddenly, I'm hungry."

Most of the creatures, suddenly more man than ant, fell back inside the fiery boundary, rolling and throwing off their formalwear. Not a few ran off down dark Midtown thoroughfares, including the one shouting the doctor's name like a curse.

Back at the theater, Dr. Franks and Stella cheered. The crowd, thinking a celebrity had arrived, cheered as well.

Dr. Franks shook Bates' hand.

"Thank you, sir. You have done humanity a great service. If there is anything I can ever do for you..."

Dr. Jive had Bates by the other arm and was pulling him toward the stage door in the alley. Bates pulled away.

"Actually man—you think you could jack that into my guitar?"

THE BASEMENT OF MRS. FRANKS

Bo Diddley something, something something ring,
[booga dooga booga dooga booga doog doog]
If that diamond ring don't shine,
[booga dooga booga dooga booga doog doog]
Wood guano break-in to a pilot nine.
[booga dooga booga dooga booga doog doog]...

Rapidly oscillating chords cannoned out of Dr. Franks' hi-fi and ricocheted around his mother's basement. The doctor himself rocked precariously on an old lawn chair, his office chair having been rolled out to the street for trash day.

If that pirate isle can't stay-ay
[booga dooga booga dooga booga doog doog]
Evil eye take a bagel from Jay.
[booga dooga booga dooga booga doog doog]
[woo wah-oo, woo-a, wah-a, woo-a, woo-a-oo]...

The doctor rocked his head as much as his concussion would allow. He liked the waffling electric sound. It reminded him of a Theremin.

Mr. Bates had given him the record as thanks for juicing up his electric guitar for *The Ed Sullivan Show* performance. The act had been a big hit, despite a typically awkward introduction by the host.

Dash, two days out of heart surgery and resting on a propped-up throw pillow, seemed to be enjoying the music as well. The squirrel's new heart, which the crypto-veterinarian had transplanted from a recently-deceased pigeon, seemed to be adapting to its new body. Dr. Franks tried not to think about the pigeon.

[woo wah-oo, woo-a, wah-a, woo-a, woo-a-oo]...

"Turn that racket down," Mrs. Frank called from upstairs. "It can't be good for your pet rat."

The doctor complied, if only to be nice. After all, it was his mother who had bailed him out of jail after that eventful Sunday melee. He took a sip of chemistry-set lemonade and closed his eyes. Yes, it had been quite a case. How ironic that he had saved the city and ended up in jail for his efforts. Ironic and typical. Such, it seemed, was the life of a homoscientist.

"Bernie, when are your friends stopping over?" his mother called. "I thought I'd heat up some TV dinners. The ones with the cobbler in its own compartment."

"Please, mother—I'm trying to recuperate."

His accomplices—Stella, Einstein and Cousin Phelps—had avoided arrest, which was one good thing. Phelpsy had gone completely off the reservation, but had taken the time to drop off an envelope with two hundred and fifty bucks. Apparently, a racing tip had finally paid off.

The record ended. All was quiet, save for the squirrel's soft breathing. Mrs. Franks, no doubt in an act of genuine concern, was refraining from running the vacuum cleaner. Dr. Franks dozed off. The concussion, the electrocution and night in the clink had worn him out.

He dreamed he was with his father, back in Africa. They were aboard the broken-down German steamer, sipping whiskey out of tin cups. His father turned to him, smiled, and said, "Good job, BERN-urd."

That's how he knew he was dreaming.

The cacophonous door chimes woke him up. He could hear his mother tromp across the floor above him and open the door.

"Jesus, what do you want?" he heard her say.

Soon there were heavy footfalls on the stairs.

What's Inspector Grimes doing here? Franks wondered.

Dr. Franks nodded at the inspector, but didn't rise. The policeman settled into the charred electric chair, depositing his frayed cigar stub in the upturned hat on his lap.

"So," he said after a long pause, "still in your mother's basement."

Dr. Franks shrugged. "Looks like."

Grimes looked around the room, first at Dash, then at the chemistry set. He fiddled with the brim of his hat.

"Are you here to arrest me again?"

"Not exactly." Grimes put the cigar in his mouth and then dropped it back in his hat. "I came to…apologize." He nearly choked on the last word.

Dr. Franks raised an eyebrow, the one that wasn't singed.

"It looks like you were, how do I put this?"

"Right?"

"Something like that."

"Did you find Flekeman? And Henna?"

Grimes shook his head. "We couldn't find that guy. And it looks like the Lovely Henna skipped town."

Dr. Franks took a long swig of lemonade, savoring it. It seemed he hadn't contracted rabies after all.

"What will you do with the survivors?"

"We're sending them to an island."

"Aruba?"

"Riker's."

There was a pause. Dash coughed and spat.

"So what you're saying is, I solved the case."

Now it was Grimes' turn to cough. "Actually, there is no case to solve. Those initial suicides—the editor, the choir director, the accountant and the comedian—turned out to be suicides. I suppose we could try to prove that that potion Dinky Dave sold pushed them to it, but—who would we pin it on? Everybody's dead or disappeared. If you think about it, the only case we have is against you."

Franks threw his head back and immediately regretted it. A donut crumb fell from his beard.

"What? The Dinky Dave murder?"

"Don't worry about that." Grimes waved a hand dismissively. "But there's breaking and entering at the lab supply store, reckless endangerment, arson—"

"Arson? I saved the city!"

"Yeah, but you also burned down the Flatiron Building."

"True."

"You're just lucky it wasn't the famous Flatiron Building designed by Louis Sullivan."

Dr. Franks' mouth dropped. "I didn't know there was another one."

Grimes stood up. Pieces of chair fell to the floor.

"But listen, I think we can sweep it all under the rug." He gave an exaggerated wink. "Sullivan put in a good word for you."

"Ed Sullivan?"

"Not to mention Steve & Edie. After all, you did save the city."

"Is there perhaps a monetary award?"

Grimes crossed to the stairs, put his cigar in his mouth and his hat on his head.

"No, but," he paused. "But perhaps down the line the department might hire you again."

Dr. Franks grinned. "As a...?"

Grimes eyed him suspiciously. "What?"

"Hire me as a...?"
Grimes ascended the steps without looking back.
"Aw, don't make me say it, doc."

EPILOGUE

Sergeant Marvin Dingle hobbled out of the Staten Island Hospital in Midtown Manhattan. His thin face, pasty on the best of days, glowed a healthy pink. And if one could have a hop in one's limp, Dingle had it. Strangely enough, the involuntary enema and ice bath had rejuvenated him. He felt good. Great, in fact. Actually, the last few weeks had been a cathartic experience. Life, he now realized, was a precious and fleeting thing. No more would he dwell on past failures or wild dreams that would never come true. From now on he, Sergeant Marvin Dibble, was going to live in the moment. Gone were the feelings of guilt and insecurity, of fear and self-hatred. He took a few steps down the sidewalk and looked around him. It was a clear autumn evening. He even thought he could see a few stars, despite the glare of the city lights. One of them, directly above him, was exceptionally bright. He made a wish. Not for himself. In his present frame of mind, he lacked for nothing. He was centered and content. No, his wish was that all the peoples of the earth could feel the peace and happiness he now felt.

The star became brighter. Flaming red-orange and throwing off faint green sparks. He smiled wanly. It was a spiritual experience, a participation in the numinous.

Then the meteorite hit him.

THE END

ABOUT THE AUTHOR

Chris Bittler has written for television, film and everything else. Raised in the mean streets of the Chicago suburbs and currently residing in Wisconsin, he doesn't know a thing about New York City.

Bittler has authored two other books: *The Bad Idea Catalog* (with Dave Markov) and *Naperville* (second-place winner in the 2013 Amazon Breakthrough Novel Award).